...... 2 TI(
GAME ON!

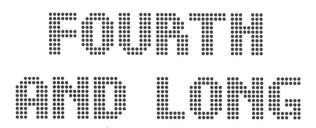

FOURTH AND LONG

STEPHEN D. SMITH with LISE CALDWELL

Standard
PUBLISHING
Bringing The Word to Life™

Cincinnati, Ohio

From Stephen

For my collaborator, Lise. Thanks for your efforts.
For my editor Greg Holder and for Diane Stortz.
Thanks to both of you for not giving up on me
even when I'd pretty much given up on myself.

From Lise

For Andrew

ISBN 0-7847-1471-1

11 10 09 08 07 06 05   9 8 7 6 5 4 3 2 1

Library of Congress Cataloging-in-Publication Data

Smith, Stephen D. (Stephen Dodd), 1961-
   Fourth and long / Stephen D. Smith with Lise Caldwell.
       p. cm.
   Summary: Seventh-grader Alex Rogers is devastated at not making the junior high foot-
ball team, but his involvement with a Bible study group and a teamwork lesson on the
paintball field help him cope.
   ISBN 0-7847-1471-1 (pbk.)
   [1. Football--Fiction. 2. Schools--Fiction. 3. Teamwork (Sports)--Fiction. 4. Friendship--
Fiction. 5. Christian life--Fiction.] I. Caldwell, Lise, 1974- II. Title.
   PZ7.S659382Fo 2005
   [Fic]--dc22
                              2005007306

CHAPTER:01

Although it was still early on a late July morning, the Oklahoma temperature had soared to ninety-two degrees and would break the one hundred mark by afternoon. Heat ripples rose from the patch of dry field grass at Muskogee Elementary School. And the scorching breeze made it hard to breathe.

Panting, Alex Rogers pushed back his damp auburn-colored hair and wiped stinging sweat from his brown eyes. He checked his players' positions. Like him, most of his buddies were seventh graders, and a few of them thought they had a shot at making the football team this year. A slim chance. Organizing pick-up games helped Alex get in as much practice as possible before football camp.

Plus it helped him prove he wasn't made of glass. It was better now, but Alex still hated how his friends acted around him. When his dad died of cancer, everyone treated him *nice*—too nice. Nobody ever teased him, laughed at him, punched him in the arm.

Alex knew he was good at this game. Everything he knew about football, his dad Frank Rogers had taught him: how to pass, how to catch, how to look for an open man. His dad had been a quarterback at Oklahoma State and led the school to a couple of bowl game victories. He was even in the running for the Heismann Trophy before an injury sidelined his career.

The thing was, Alex knew he *was* different now. He'd been through something none of his buddies had. He just didn't like being *treated* differently.

Today, Alex thought, it would be different.

"Hut...hut...hike!" Alex called out as he looked at his best friend Jeff Williams, who he'd known since kindergarten. Jeff was prepared to push through the offensive line and grab the ball out of Alex's hands as soon as the center passed it to him. His buddy was muscular and already looked more like an eighth-grader. And Jeff was the only friend who didn't treat Alex like he was the one with some terrible disease.

Freckle-faced Scott Humphries, the center, hiked the ball to Alex and then pushed forward against the charging defensive line. Alex shuffled backwards and scanned the field for his receivers.

Both Chuck Ryan and Dan Tenkiller were open. But Dan had a longer reach. Plus the sun-browned Cherokee stood a head taller than anyone else. With

Jeff closing in, Alex zeroed in on Dan and released the ball, sending it spiraling through the air.

"Look out!" the fireplug-shaped Chuck called to Dan, as he watched the ball fall toward his teammate. But Dan was concentrating so much on the ball, he failed to see the defensive back crouching in mid-run, who plowed into Dan. The ball hit the ground and bounced and rolled onto the sidelines.

"What's the problem?" Alex yelled. "Can't you catch a ball?" Dan's eyes opened wide in shock. Alex was surprised at the anger in his own voice.

Fine, he thought. *Maybe if they get mad at me they'll stop treating me like a baby.*

It worked.

"Hey, Dude!" Chuck yelled. He looked ready for a fight. "I was wide open. Lay off Dan! Next time look at all your options."

Alex's anger and frustration made him feel stronger and more powerful somehow. More alive than he'd felt since his dad died.

"Hey!" Alex said. "Don't tell me how to play the game. You were both wide open when I threw the ball." Alex knew Chuck was right, but it felt good to yell.

Everybody looked at one another, frowning, but no one said anything to Alex. Slowly, they regrouped where the ball had fallen. Without full teams, everyone played both offense and defense. Jeff now quarterbacked for his team. The offense lined up, and the center readied the ball for a snap to the QB.

As a defensive tackle, Alex took his position in front of Matt Goodman, a tall scrawny red-headed kid, whom Alex thought looked like the scarecrow in the *Wizard of Oz*.

Jeff called for the ball and grabbed it. Alex charged as hard as he could toward Matt, knocking him to the ground. Winded, Matt lay in the brittle grass and rubbed his aching shoulder. Alex rushed toward Jeff in an attempt to stop him before the ball was thrown. Too late! Jeff got off his pass.

The ball hurtled toward Craig Hashimoto, an eighth-grader, who looked back over his shoulder from the thirty-yard line. Craig caught the pass and sprinted toward the goal before the defense could stop him. When he reached the end zone, Craig held the ball high and did a little dance. His buddies cheered!

Not Alex. His stomach still churned with anger. It had felt good to plow into Matt. Alex's anger scared him a little. Standing now, Matt grimaced as he rubbed his shoulder.

"You okay?" Alex asked.

"Yeah, I'm okay, but take it easy next time. You could do some real damage." Matt turned his back on Alex and ambled over to the sidelines, where he plopped down to watch Jeff kick the extra point. In their middle school league, quarterbacks doubled as kickers.

As Alex watched the ball sail into the end zone, past a stake they had set up to mark the goal, he took a swig of water. It dribbled down his chin onto his sweat-stained T-shirt. Man, it was hot!

When he noticed the other guys avoiding him and gathering around Matt, Alex started to wonder if he'd overdone the tough-guy act. Sure, he didn't want to be treated like a baby, but he didn't want to lose all his friends, either.

"Let's call it quits," Jeff said, his eyes blazing as he walked up to Alex. "It's getting too hot to play anyway." Alex knew Jeff was upset with him.

"What?" Alex said. "Are you kidding? Football camp starts next week and it's in full gear. You think this is hot, just wait."

"That's the point," Jeff said. "Let's wait until then to get heat stroke. I wanna hit the pool before it gets crowded."

"Fine," Alex said, dropping down on the dry grass. "I'll stay here and practice my kicking."

Alex just had to make the football team. It was what his dad had wanted. Sure, seventh graders almost never made it. And yeah, Alex knew the competition was tough. But *no one* wanted to be on the Eisenhower Middle School football team more than

Alex Rogers.

Jeff flopped down next to Alex, beads of sweat dripping down his face. "What's your problem today?" Jeff asked. "First you lose it with Dan and Chuck, then you practically dislocate Matt's shoulder, and now you wanna blow off going to the pool."

Alex avoided Jeff's eyes and watched a golden retriever trotting through the schoolyard, with its tongue lolling out.

"Well?" Jeff asked.

"I'm sick of everybody feeling sorry for me," Alex said.

"With an attitude like that, no one's going to."

"Fine with me," Alex said. He knew he sounded like a jerk, but he didn't care.

Jeff was quiet for a minute and then stood up. Suddenly, his grinned turned evil and Alex knew he was in trouble.

"You know what I'll have to do if you keep this up," Jeff said.

Alex tried not to smile, but he couldn't help it. "No," he said. "What?"

"The only thing I can do when you start acting like a total jerk," Jeff said, with mock seriousness.

"No, not—"

"Shin kicking!" they both yelled at the same time.

Alex stood up as fast as he could, but Jeff had

already landed a solid kick. Oklahoma clay dust flew in both their faces as they shuffled around on the sidelines, kicking out with their worn-out sneakers. Laughing, Alex gave as good as he got. The other guys rooted them on. It had been a long time since Alex had let loose and had this much fun.

Soon Alex and Jeff were in too much pain and laughing too hard to keep up the fight.

"Come on, you two morons," Chuck said. "Let's get to the pool before it's too crowded."

As they gathered up their stuff to walk home, Jeff shoved Alex and said, "At least you got your kicking practice in."

Alex shoved him back and laughed.

Alex headed home to change clothes and grab his pool pass. This was the first summer his mom had let him go to the pool without her tagging along.

"Lifeguards aren't parents," she'd said when he was younger.

Last summer they had only gone to the pool a couple of times because of Dad. Mostly, they had spent their time at the hospital or at the house when they brought Frank Rogers home to die.

Alex tried not to think about it. He shivered after barging through the door. It was freezing! His mom loved air-conditioning. Alex headed for the hallway.

"Don't walk on my clean floor in those filthy sneakers!" his mom called from the living room.

He stopped and kicked off his shoes, muttering under his breath. "Mothers must have X-ray vision."

"Yep," she said, startling him as she rounded the corner. "Along with super hearing."

Dressed in a worn pair of khaki shorts and a sleeveless pink blouse, Mom had pulled back her hair into a ponytail. Alex thought it made her look like a teenager, but he didn't say anything.

"Hey, Mom."

"Hey, yourself," she said eyeing his dust-encrusted jeans and T-shirt.

"The guys and me are going swimming," he said, running up the stairs toward his room.

"The guys and I," she shouted up at him automatically. Mom was a high school English teacher. "Take a shower before you go. You look like a farmer."

Half the time Alex didn't know what she was talking about, but it was great to have her home. Since she was a teacher, she got summers off. Supposedly. In reality, she spent a lot of her time preparing for the fall semester. Alex just prayed he never had to take one of her classes. Now *that* was a scary thought!

After taking a shower and grabbing his swim trunks, Alex stopped in the living room to let his mother know he was leaving. She sat cross-legged on the carpet, with folders and notebooks spread all around her.

"I'm leaving for the pool, Mom," he said.

"Do you have your pass?" she asked, circling something in red on a folder. She didn't even look up.

"Yes."

"Sunscreen?"

"Yessss!"

"Water-wings?"

"Mom!"

Peeking up at him, she kidded, "I could send the ducky float ring instead. All the guys have them."

"I don't think so," Alex said.

His mother sighed. "Life was so much easier when all I had to do was put water-wings on you to keep you safe. By the way, Sara will be at the pool today too. Keep an eye on her for me, will you?"

Sara was Alex's ten-year-old sister. And the biggest pain in the world. "Aw, Mom!"

"She went with Carmen Rodriguez and her dad."

"I guess I can keep an eye on her . . . if I have to." Alex tried to sound reluctant, but he was excited. Carmen's dad was the school's football coach.

"I thought that might get your attention."

She tried not to smile, but couldn't help it. Alex rolled his brown eyes and banged out the front door.

The pool was already crowded when Alex arrived.

He flashed his pass at the girl sitting behind the high counter, who barely glanced up from her teen magazine. She waved him in, and he quickly walked across the wet floor of the men's locker room and out onto the sun-blinding pool deck.

Alex put his shades back on and scanned the crowd for Coach Rodriguez. He saw Jeff first, who waved him over, but then Alex spotted Coach about thirty feet to Jeff's right. Coach wasn't hard to miss with his deep tan, dark-brown moustache, and muscular build. Alex signaled to Jeff, but then headed straight for his little sister Sara and the Coach.

Giggling, Sara and Carmen sat together on a green and yellow beach towel. They smelled like Coppertone and chlorine. Coach Rodriguez lounged in a plastic chair nearby.

"Hi, Sis," Alex said. "I just came by to make sure you brought your sunblock." He raised his voice slightly to make sure Coach knew he was there.

"Hey, Weirdo," Sara said, squeezing water out of her dark brown pigtails. "Why are you yelling? And since when do you care if I get sunburned?"

"Since Mom wanted me to check on you," he said, sarcastically.

"Really?" she asked, raising her voice too. "I thought maybe it was because the *football coach* just happens to be sitting next to me."

Alex could have strangled her. There really had to be a reasonable legal defense for the murder of an obnoxious little sister. But instead he just glared at her and turned to walk away. Alex bumped into Raf Rodriguez, the coach's son, who had just emerged from the pool. Raf raked back his wet dark-brown curly hair with dripping hands.

"What's your hurry, Man?" Raf asked.

"Sorry, Raf. Just trying to escape my sister."

"Alex? I didn't recognize you. You've grown a foot taller since last fall when you and your mom came over to pick up Sara."

Alex had always looked up to Raf. Eisenhower High hadn't seen a quarterback like the coach's son for a long time. Tall, lean, and muscular, he'd already broken several state records by the end of his junior year. He'd be a senior this year and at the top of his game. Sports reporters had already interviewed Raf several times for the paper, and it was rumored college scouts had already taken a look at him.

Even though the high school quarterback was treated like a king in this football crazy town, Raf never let it go to his head. He'd even helped organize a kick-a-thon fundraiser at his church to help pay for Frank Rogers's medical bills.

Suddenly, Raf yelped and leaped off his feet. While he and Alex had been talking, Carmen had snuck up behind her big brother and dropped an ice cube down the back of his swim trunks. She squealed as he turned to grab her, but Carmen and Sara evaded his reach and splashed into the pool.

Laughing, Coach Rodriguez stood up and came over to Alex and Raf. "I know it doesn't seem like it now, guys, but someday you'll both be thankful to have little sisters."

Alex didn't want to disagree with the coach, but couldn't imagine that ever happening.

"Dad's been saying that to me for years," Raf said. "I'm still waiting for *someday*."

"So, Alex," Coach Rodriguez said. "Are you coming to football camp?"

"Absolutely!"

"You know what the best thing is about football camp?" Coach asked, putting his arm over Alex's shoulder.

Alex wasn't sure what to answer. He wanted to say something like, "Having the opportunity to learn about the greatest sport ever invented from a fine coach like you," but he thought that might be over the top.

Coach answered his own question. "No sisters," he said. "I'm going to get a drink. See you two later."

After Coach Rodriguez walked away, Raf asked Alex, "Do you think you have a shot at making the team?"

Alex didn't want to sound too confident. "I've been playing football since I was old enough to walk, and I've been practicing a lot this summer with my friends over at Muskogee elementary."

Suddenly, Alex thought about his dad. Raf must have been thinking about the same thing. "If you can play anything like your dad," Raf said, "you'll be the best quarterback the school's ever seen."

Alex didn't know what to say. He loved that his dad was such a good player, but he was afraid he'd never measure up.

"If you and your friends want me to," Raf said, "I'd be happy to drop by tomorrow and watch you— maybe show you some plays."

"Cool! That'd be great! Thanks, Raf."

Jeff sauntered toward Alex, looking annoyed.

"Well, I've gotta get going, Raf," Alex said.

"I'll see you tomorrow morning at practice."

Jeff, Matt, Craig, and Chuck moved toward Alex. They'd already been swimming for more than a half hour. None of them looked happy.

"Didn't you see me wave you over?" Jeff asked.

"Yeah, but Mom wanted me to check on Sara."

"Who just *happened* to be sitting next to Coach," Chuck said, planting his fists on his hips.

"Yeah," Alex admitted. He changed the subject. "Guess what? Raf offered to come watch our game in the morning and give us some pointers."

"No kidding!" said Jeff, his expression brightening.

"Yeah, that's just dandy," said Chuck, red-faced. "But if you and Coach stay all buddy-buddy, you won't need any pointers to get on the team." The sturdy kid turned and cannon-balled into the water, splashing them all.

"What's his problem?" Alex asked.

"He thinks you're trying to use your friendship with Coach and Raf to get on the team," scarecrow Matt said. "Coach only takes one seventh grader a year. Everybody knows that. If it's going to be you, no one else has a chance—not Chuck, not Jeff, not me."

Alex didn't say anything, but thought that after seeing how skinny Matt looked in swim trunks, Coach sure wasn't going to pick the tall redhead. Matt's bird legs looked like Popsicle sticks.

"I think it's great Raf's coming tomorrow," Jeff said. "That's going to help all of us do better in football tryouts, not just Alex. Chuck will get over it."

"He always does," Matt said before jumping back in the pool. Jeff followed.

"You coming, Alex?" Jeff said, dog-paddling and clearing water out of his nose.

"In a minute. My foot hurts."

Alex sat down in one of the white plastic deck chairs to check the bottom of his foot for a splinter. It had been bothering him since this morning. *Probably just a stone bruise*, he thought. Suddenly, a shadow came between him and the sun.

"Hi," a girl's sweet voice said.

Alex looked up at Heidi Hendricks, who sat down in the chair next to him.

"Hey," he said.

Alex knew Heidi from church—when he still went to church—before his dad died. She was a little strange. Heidi was the first to memorize all the Bible verses, answer every question the Sunday school teacher asked, and always offered to pray for everybody. Even before Alex decided he was mad at God, church had become kind of a drag. But Heidi seemed to love it.

Heidi always looked a little strange too. Her clothes were usually a little out of style, and her thick curly-red hair frizzed, especially in the rain. Alex had to admit though that she looked better today than he'd ever seen her. She was wearing a one-piece green swimsuit that brought out the green in her eyes, and she looked taller than at the end of sixth grade.

"Haven't seen you at church for awhile," she said.

"Yeah, well, God stopped listening to me, so I stopped talking to him," Alex said.

Heidi chewed on her bottom lip and seemed

uncertain what to say. She finally asked, "How's your summer going?"

"Okay, I guess. Football camp starts soon. I plan on making the team when school starts."

"That's neat," she said.

Alex looked up and saw Raf waving in their direction. Alex waved back, but Raf kept waving like he didn't see Alex. Heidi turned to see who he was looking at. When she saw Raf, she smiled broadly and waved at him. Raf grinned and gave her a thumbs-up sign.

What's that all about? Alex thought.

Heidi seemed to read his mind. "Raf and I went on a missions trip together to Mexico earlier this summer. A bunch of kids from church helped build a house for a pastor and his family down there."

Alex should have known it had something to do with church. "How come? Aren't there plenty of poor people here?"

Heidi ignored Alex's sarcasm. "Sure, but Mr. Rodriguez wanted to take Raf and Carmen to the village where their grandfather had been born and raised. So he organized the trip and opened it up to anyone in the youth group who wanted to go."

At the mention of Coach Rodriguez, Alex's interest perked up.

"We're so blessed here," Heidi said. "You can't

imagine how some people have to live—a whole family in a one-room shack with a dirt floor. No bathroom or running water. It really made me grateful for what we have. I wanna go back sometime."

"Really?" Alex asked.

"Yeah," Heidi said. "Even though it was a long trip in a church bus. And you think it's hot here! It was a hundred and twenty in the shade in Mexico."

"Bugs and snakes?"

"Everywhere," she answered, shivering.

"Cool!" Alex said.

As he continued to listen to Heidi talk about the trip, he forgot what an oddball she was. Actually, she was pretty funny, especially when she told him about Raf trying to use his two year's worth of Spanish class to talk to his great-aunt Esperanza.

"Raf spilled paint all over himself one day," Heidi said. "Then he said to his aunt, '*Estoy muy embarazada.*' He thought he was saying 'I am very embarrassed.'"

"What did he say?" Alex asked.

"'I am very pregnant!' Heidi giggled.

Alex burst out laughing. Several people nearby looked over at them, and Alex suddenly felt uncomfortable. Tons of kids from school were at the pool that day. He didn't want them thinking he was some kind of religious nut job like Heidi.

To his great relief, Heidi stood up and said, "It's

about time for my mom to pick me up. See ya."

"Yeah, later."

"Look, Alex, I know you're not really interested in church right now, but if you'd like to drop by youth group some Wednesday night, I think you'd really enjoy it. I'd be happy to sit with you."

That was the last thing Alex wanted. Maybe Heidi *liked* him or something. Maybe that was why she was being so friendly. But as weird as she was, Alex didn't want to hurt her feelings.

"Okay, I'll think about it," he said. "See ya."

Then he jumped into the pool before she had time to respond. He swam over to where the guys were playing water volleyball and took a place on Jeff's team. In between plays, Jeff asked, "Was that Heidi Hendricks you were talking to?"

"Yeah," said Alex. "She's such a whacko."

"Yeah," Jeff said. "I hardly recognized her."

"She did look almost—"

"Pretty?" Jeff asked.

"I was going to say *normal*. Pretty seems like a stretch to me. Why? Do you like her or something?"

"No way!" Jeff said. But his cheeks flushed pinker, even though his face was already sunburned. Jeff served the ball and dropped the subject.

CHAPTER:02

Alex soon forgot all about Heidi and her good deeds. His mind tracked on only one topic—football. Just as he promised, Raf dropped by their scrimmage at the elementary school the next morning wearing black shorts and a gold T-shirt. He mostly just watched and cheered on the seventh graders.

But when the heat finally brought their game to a halt, Raf had a few pointers for them.

"Jeff, try loosening up a little while you're preparing to rush," Raf said. "If you aren't so stiff when you charge in, you'll be less likely to hurt yourself."

Jeff acknowledged the advice, nodding his head in understanding. "Thanks, I'll remember that."

Raf then reminded Chuck and Dan not to worry about letting the quarterback know they were open by jumping up and down.

"A good QB will know where you are," he told them. "You don't want to draw the other team's attention to you so they can intercept your pass."

Then Raf looked at Alex. Putting his arm around the younger player, Raf pointed toward the dry grass field and said, "If you want to be a quarterback like my dad says your dad was, you need to look at this field the same way you'd look at the game of 'Risk.'

"This is your empire," Raf continued, waving his hand around the closer half of the field. "That," he said, now pointing to the opposite end of the field, "is the empire you want to conquer. Lead your team like a general leading his army into battle."

"I never thought of it that way," Alex said, nodding as he surveyed the battlefield. "Thanks, Raf."

"No problemo," Raf said, smiling. "You've gotta lot of good moves, Alex. Just keep practicing."

Raf turned to gangly Matt Goodman. "And you, my man, have a pretty accurate aim, but you need more control. Remember to cock your arm, keep your eye on your receiver, and then follow through. Let the momentum carry the ball down the field to your target."

"You're right," Matt said. "Sometimes I get to thinking about where everybody else is, and I hesitate."

Alex didn't know why, but he felt a little jealous that Raf was talking to Matt about the quarterback position. Everybody knew that Alex was the QB on this team. As Raf continued to give advice and kid around with everyone, Alex turned and left. He didn't even say goodbye. And frankly, he just didn't care what his friends thought.

On Friday night Alex ran into Heidi again at the video store. He'd ridden his bike over to pick up a DVD, but he couldn't find anything that he, his mom, and Sara would all like. He usually just scoped out the new releases, but out of desperation he wandered into the "family" section.

"*Bambi* is always a good choice," said a voice next to him. It was Heidi.

The weirdness at the pool came rushing back. Alex wanted to get rid of her—fast.

"Yeah, well, I'm kind of avoiding movies that deal with the death of parents right now," he said.

Heidi looked mortified. "Alex, I'm so sorry. I didn't mean . . . I wasn't thinking. I'm such an idiot!"

Now it was Alex's turn to feel bad. "Heidi, it's okay. I was just joking."

"You sure have a twisted sense of humor," she said and changed the subject. "Have you seen *Princess Diaries*? It's really funny."

"You're kidding, right? That's a chick flick."

"I bet your mom and Sara would like it," Heidi said. "And you might surprise yourself."

"Not enough action for me," he said.

Heidi shifted her sandaled feet and took a deep

breath. "Listen, we're having a movie night at church on Sunday. Big screen, popcorn, soft drinks, Jujubes, the works. You wanna come?"

Alex couldn't figure out why Heidi didn't get the picture. He was definitely not interested in church or her. "I can't," he said. "Football camp starts the next day, and I really need to get a good night's sleep."

"Sure," Heidi said, "maybe some other time. Guess I'll see you later. Mom's ready to check out."

"Later," Alex said. He took *Princess Diaries* off the shelf and read the jacket cover. Maybe it wouldn't be too bad. At least Mom and Sara would enjoy it. He kept it as a "possible" while he looked through the other titles.

The rotten thing was, Alex *didn't* get a good night's sleep that Sunday night. He just stared at his ceiling for hours, thinking about football camp. He just had to do well. He had to show Coach Rodriguez that he was the best seventh grader out there—that he could play like his dad.

It was two in the morning before Alex finally drifted off to sleep. When the alarm went off at seven-thirty, he groaned. His eyes felt all scratchy— like they were full of grit. After a shower, he some- how managed to get dressed and eat breakfast, but he was exhausted and grouchy.

"Good luck!" his mom said as she handed him his water bottle.

"Yeah, whatever," Alex said. He half waved at her and slouched out the door to climb on his bike.

Jeff met him halfway down the block. "You ready for this, bud?" he asked, riding his bike in circles.

"I'm ready to get it over with and start practicing with the team," Alex answered. He knew he sounded cocky, but his heart was racing and his palms were sweating. He was afraid of failing and disappointing the memory of his dad. He just *had* to make the team.

Alex noticed that Jeff let the macho comment slide. *Now he's even treating me weird.*

When the two friends arrived at the middle school football field, they locked their bikes on the racks next to the bleachers. They were about fifteen minutes early. But Raf was already hauling out the gear. Alex saw him first.

"Let me give you a hand with that, Raf!" he shouted across the field.

Alex trotted toward Raf, with Jeff trailing behind. As all three lugged the canvas ball bags and several blocking sleds out onto the field, Alex tried to think of something to say to Raf. Then he remembered what Heidi had told him.

"I hear you went to Mexico," Alex said.

"Yeah, man, it was incredible," Raf said. The senior smiled. "We built a house for the minister of a small church down there. And we led a Vacation Bible

School for the kids in the village. I even got to teach them a little football, or *futbol american* as they call it."

"Did you really?" Jeff asked, his blue eyes excited. "That sounds awesome!"

"It really was," Raf said, turning to Jeff. "You can't really begin to understand how much we have here until you go someplace like that."

Alex felt irritated. This was supposed to be his time to hang out with Raf, and Jeff was butting in.

By that time, everybody was coming on to the field. Dan and Chuck. Scott and Craig. Matt too. And a bunch of eight graders. Matt looked over at Raf and waved. Raf grinned at him. Was Matt trying to make points with Raf so he'd get picked for the team? Alex didn't have time to figure it out, because Coach came on the field and blew his whistle.

"Welcome to football camp," Coach said when they all gathered around him. "For some of you, this will be the hardest week of your life. But football is a tough sport, and you have to be tough to play it. It's also a team sport. I want to see your skill, but I'm also looking for how well you work with others.

"This morning we'll rotate around the field clockwise to various stations, where we'll assess your skills. But first Raf will lead you in some warm-up exercises. Raf? You want to add anything?"

"Nope," Raf said. "Let's get started."

Sultry humid air hung like a thick white haze on the horizon, and tall white clouds threatened thunderstorms later in the day once it really heated up. After Raf had the guys run wind-sprints, Alex could already feel the sweat trickling down his back and soaking through his T-shirt.

Next Coach split the boys into five groups of six and sent them to the different stations around the field. Matt and Alex were in the same group.

"So you think you have a chance?" Alex asked, drinking water from his sports bottle.

"I don't know," Matt said. "As much as anybody else, I guess. I love to play, but I don't really know the game as well as I should. Raf convinced me to at least give it a shot."

Their group went to one end of the field where the blocking sleds waited for them. Alex had seen one before, but he'd never worked with it. His dad had always told him the blocking sled was a real killer. Assistant Coach Benson, who was short, bald, and chubby, was in charge of this exercise.

"Okay, fellas, line up. And get ready to fall down," he said.

A few of the eighth-grade boys laughed. Coach Benson showed their group how to prepare for impact, and how to push once their shoulders had nested in the pad.

"It doesn't look all that hard," Chuck said.

"Yeah, if you're a pro," Craig Hashimoto said. "Tell me how you feel after you hit the ground."

Coach Benson blew his whistle and Alex charged his sled. He thought he was ready for the impact, but when he hit hard, he was knocked backward. His face flushed with embarrassment. Chuck had planted his legs and hit the blocking sled with full force, but he dropped like a rock too. Only Matt was still standing.

"Great job, Goodman!" Coach Benson said. "Sometimes the lean ones are the scrappiest. Let's try this again, shall we, gentlemen?"

He blew his whistle and again they charged. This time, Alex held his ground, but the sled refused to budge. In frustration, Alex punched it.

"Watch it, Rogers," Coach Benson said. "Broken fingers won't get you anything but a cast on your hand.

Over the course of the next two hours, they worked their way around the field. Alex worked harder than he ever had that day. He wanted to show Coach Rodriguez just how committed he was. But whenever he looked at Coach, Coach was watching someone else. Usually Jeff or Matt.

Finally Alex's group made it to the passing station, where Coach Rodriguez was supervising this one himself. And passing was Alex's best skill.

Alex loved the way the football felt in his hand.

He had his dad's long fingers, which naturally cradled the ball. When it was his turn, Alex hurled his arm forward, pushing the ball through the air, releasing it, and watching its perfect arc as it spun like a missile toward its calculated target. Craig ran forward to receive the ball, but it hit the ground behind him. Alex slumped his shoulders in defeat. *Hashimoto should have caught it.*

"Fine job, Alex," Coach Rodriguez said. "Nice form. Now we just need to increase your distance." Coach began to tell Alex how he could get more distance from his throw, but Alex didn't hear a word he said. What could Coach teach him that his father hadn't already shown him a million times?

Finally, the day was over. Alex and Jeff rode their bikes into Braum's parking lot and locked them up. Alex could already taste the double-dip chocolate-mint waffle cone. The electric doors swhoosed open, and they joined the long line at the ice cream counter.

The guys waited patiently for their cones. After they'd been served, they slid into one of the large booths and licked their cones in silence for awhile, until there was no longer any danger of it dripping down the sides.

"Man, what's better than Braum's!" Jeff sighed.

"Nothing short of heaven," Alex said. "I hope they've got Braum's up there. Dad and I used to come here every Saturday afternoon."

Jeff was uncomfortably silent.

"What?" Alex said.

"Nothin'."

Alex stared at Jeff for a moment and then realized what was wrong. "I can't even talk about my dad without you going all quiet on me?"

"No, it's okay," Jeff said. "It's just that it's been a long time since . . . " His voice trailed off.

"Since what?"

"Since you've talked about him."

Alex felt the anger rise in his chest. "I wish you guys would stop treating me like I died!"

"Hey, man," Jeff said. "I'm sorry. I didn't mean anything."

Alex looked around at the people in the other booths and glared. Four older guys at another table turned their heads away quickly.

Trying to change the subject, Jeff said, "I thought you did really great today."

Alex bit into the waffle cone and calmed down a little. "Yeah, it felt good."

"You're a cinch to get picked by Coach," Jeff said.

"You think so?"

"It's in the bag," Jeff said. "Hey, you wanna watch a DVD at my house tonight?"

"Nah, I think I'll hit the sack early. I'm wiped."

"Yeah, me too."

The two best friends finished their ice cream in silence and wiped sticky fingers on a pile of napkins.

Later they parted at Alex's driveway. "See ya tomorrow," Jeff said, riding away.

"Same time, same place."

When Alex unlocked the door, he walked into a quiet house. Mom had left a note, saying that she and Sara had gone grocery shopping.

Wearily, he climbed the stairs and didn't even bother to take a shower. He was bone tired. So he just collapsed on his bed and slept the rest of the afternoon.

After dinner, Alex was still tired and cranky. While Mom and Sara watched television, he said goodnight and went to bed early. But just like the night before, sleep wouldn't come. He folded his hands behind his head and watched the lightning flash across the stark white ceiling.

Alex went over and over every mistake he had made today and vowed to do better tomorrow. He just had to make the team. He just had to.

The next three days were just as tough, but Alex thought he was doing well. On Friday a real scrimmage would show what all of them could do. Alex just hoped his friends would really let him play instead of babying him the way they'd done all summer. He didn't want Coach to think he was a slacker.

By the end of the week, though, Alex was really worn out. He still wasn't sleeping much, and his nerves wouldn't let him eat more than a few bites at each meal. His mom looked worried, but she didn't say anything.

After the short rainstorm at the first of the week, it had gotten even hotter and more humid. When Alex ran wind-sprints the next morning, he was already sweating profusely and could smell his own stink. Raf called a five-minute break, and Alex dropped down on the grass.

"You look awful, Alex," Dan said, standing over him

"Thanks," Alex said sarcastically.

"Maybe you should tell Coach you need to sit out this morning," Craig added, looking well-rested.

"Craig, if you don't shut your trap, you'll be the one sitting out this morning!" Alex answered.

"Okay, already!" Craig said, turning beet-red. "Sorry I cared."

Raf soon called them back together and divided the large group up into teams again. Alex was grouped with his practice buddies Jeff, Chuck, Matt, Craig, and a couple of other eight graders. Dan was split into another group.

"Matt, you'll quarterback," Raf told him.

Alex rolled his light-brown eyes. He didn't get it! What made Matt so special? If Alex wasn't allowed to quarterback during camp, he'd never be able to demonstrate his skills for Coach.

The scrimmage got underway, with Alex playing the tight end position. Trying for a first down, Matt threw a pass to their running back Jeff. Alex didn't think the ball was going to make it, so he raced to receive it before Jeff could make the catch. Alex leaped up and touched the football with just the tips of his fingers, but it was too high for him. He fumbled it.

The whistle blew, and the team regrouped. Jeff waited until he was alone with Alex to take him on. "What were you thinking?" he asked. "That ball was meant for me. I had it!"

"I just thought—" Alex began.

"You just thought it was your chance to show off for Coach again!" Jeff angrily ran his fingers through his damp hair and looked at Alex in disgust.

Alex didn't have time to respond before Coach said, "Okay, switch positions. Alex, you're the quarterback this time."

Alex nodded. Finally, his chance. The players fell into formation on opposing sides of the line and prepared for scrimmage.

As Jeff squatted down to hike the ball, he lifted his face to stare into the eyes of a friend named Nick

McNabb, a burly eight-grader, who was readying himself to push through the line and sack the quarterback.

"Go easy on him," Jeff mouthed to Nick. His friend nodded in acknowledgement.

"Hut, Hut, Hike!" Alex called as he shifted back and fourth on his heels. The ball catapulted from Jeff's hands back to the waiting grasp of Alex who jogged backwards to get a better view of Matt and Craig. Craig was faster, but the other team knew he was the obvious target for the quarterback, so they pursued Craig, leaving Matt wide open.

Alex hesitated before coiling his shoulder to prepare the throw. As he did, he saw Nick run around Jeff, heading straight for him. But Jeff pivoted on his heel and lunged at Nick, knocking him over. The ball launched clumsily from Alex's grasp and wobbled toward Matt, who ran forward and tried to catch it. He missed and the ball hit him in the helmet, rolling onto the ground. A whistle blew.

Alex looked downfield at Matt as the coach clapped and shouted "good effort" to the tall red-head. Alex was not pleased. Not with Matt's effort, and not with the lack of aggression shown by the opposing players.

"What was that, Nick?" Alex snapped. "You could have had me easy. You ran right into Jeff's arms. You let him tackle you." He could feel his face, already hot from the Oklahoma sun, turning scarlet with anger. "Why do you guys treat me like I'm going to break if you tackle me?" he asked. "I'm not some mama's boy like Matt. You can bring on the pain."

Coach Rodriguez blew the whistle.

"Come on, guys," Coach shouted. "Again."

Alex couldn't see the embarrassment on Matt's face, but Jeff, Craig, and the other guys could. So could the coach.

Alex fumed. He wasn't going to take this anymore. He again called for the snap, but this time, instead of moving back and passing, he ran across the back of the defensive line and out into the field. He was going for the goal himself. With adrenaline pumping, Alex pushed himself to run faster.

As Alex progressed down the marked ten-yard lines, an opposing defensive lineman lunged at him, but Alex rammed him with his shoulder, causing the kid to fall to the ground. Another player ran into him, but Alex extended an elbow, catching the pursuer in the chest and knocking him down. Another player ran directly into Alex from the opposite side, catching him by surprise. Alex fell hard on the baked grass field.

"Now that was a play," Alex shouted as he jumped up and danced on his toes. He hurt like crazy, but he wasn't about to let anybody know it. "See, I can take it." Alex pounded on his chest with his right fist and looked toward Jeff.

"I'll tell you what you can take, you jerk," Matt said. He walked up fast, towering over Alex. "You can take our friendship and shove it."

"What's wrong with you?" Alex said.

"I'm talking about calling me a mama's boy to make you look better," Matt said. "I don't need friends like you."

Coach blew his whistle. "Okay, guys, cool it! I think that's enough for today. It's been a good week of camp. Go home. Get some rest."

Alex picked up his water bottle and squirted it on his hair, face, and neck. As hot as it was outside, he was hotter inside. He felt like he was burning up with anger and frustration.

"Alex," Coach said. "Could I see you for a minute?"

Alex walked over to him. "Yeah, Coach?"

"You've done a really good job this week," he said.

"Thanks!" Alex said, brightening a little.

"But you really need to work on playing as a team member. Okay?"

Alex's smile froze in place. "Okay," he said. *As long as I make the team.*

CHAPTER:03

School in Muskogee started in mid-August, a week and a half after the end of football camp. The temperature hovered around the one hundred degree mark, and it looked like the weather pattern was sticking around for awhile. Oklahoma was fortunate. Texas was suffering a major drought.

Eisenhower Middle School's ancient air-conditioning system ran constantly, but still it couldn't dispel the sticky heat that seemed to envelop every classroom. Alex had always done well in school, but it was all he could do to concentrate as sweat trickled down the back of his neck. At least he never had to study much. He remembered everything he heard, which helped, because he rarely did his reading.

The first day of school usually gave Alex a major case of the jitters. Even though he wasn't a straight-A student, he still wanted to do well. He knew it was stupid to worry. But he hated learning new routines.

And he was sure he'd be the idiot who would walk into the wrong math class and realize it halfway through.

But today those worries didn't even cross his mind. Because it wasn't just the first day of school, it was the day of football tryouts.

Alex ran into Jeff at his locker after school, and they walked toward the gym to change. He hadn't seen much of his best friend since football camp. Jeff was unusually quiet, but Alex figured it was just nerves.

"Hey, man. What's up? Alex asked.

"I don't want to talk about it," Jeff answered.

"Come on. Give."

"Give? You really wanna know?" Jeff stopped. He turned to Alex and his piercing eyes stared a hole through his best friend. "Okay, I know you've been through some awful stuff. But I'm sick of feeling sorry for you. I'm sick of putting up with your lousy attitude. I'm sick of feeling guilty that my life is normal and you're the one with—"

"The dead dad," Alex said, finishing the sentence.

"See, I can't even say it!" Jeff said. "I feel like such a jerk for even thinking that you've been acting like a jerk. But Alex, you really have!"

"What's that supposed to mean?" Alex asked.

"You're happy to be my best friend until Raf shows up, then you follow him around like some puppy dog. You show off and act tough every time Coach Rodriguez is in the same hemisphere. I know it's really important for you to make the football team. I just hope it's more important than our friendship . . . because that's just about over." Jeff spun around and took off down the hallway before Alex could even respond.

Alex felt like he'd been punched in the stomach. Jeff had always been his best friend—ever since kindergarten. Jeff was the most reliable, stable person in his life. Or had been. His mom was great, but he had to be strong for her. Sara was a major pest. He'd counted on Jeff to be there for him, and he figured Jeff would always understand.

Now it looked like Jeff had abandoned him, too, just like Dad. *I can't think about this right now!* But Jeff's words kept ringing in his ears. Had Alex really made football more important than their friendship?

Alex changed in the locker room, along with some of the other guys, but he wasn't in any mood to talk. When Alex walked onto the field, Jeff was already there but ignored him.

Coach blew his whistle. "Welcome to football tryouts, gentlemen. This afternoon we'll run some drills, as well as test your endurance. Some of you will be called back for more tryouts tomorrow to help determine the position you might play. I hope you all do your very best. Now let's get started!"

Alex barely heard a word. He couldn't stop thinking about what Jeff had said. He went through the
tryouts mechanically, unable to focus. He kept shak-
ing himself, but his mind whirled with thoughts
about Jeff and Mom and Dad. What would his dad
think of him if he blew football tryouts?

"Rogers!" Coach Benson said at one point. "Are
you with us?"

"What?" Alex said.

"I *said* huddle up."

"Sorry," Alex muttered and hurried over to join
the group.

Between the Oklahoma heat and the empty pit
in his gut, Alex felt like he'd blown his last chance
for the team.

That night, Alex just stared at his plate, pushing
the hamburger casserole around with his fork, ignor-
ing his mother and sister. Sara had been carrying on
about those jeans again, and he'd just tuned out.

"Alex?" Mom asked.

"Huh?"

"I just asked how tryouts went."

"Okay, I guess."

"You don't sound very enthusiastic," Mom said.

"I don't know. A lot of guys are trying out. And

Coach usually just picks one seventh grader."

"Well, if you're meant to be on the team, you will be," she said.

"Hey, Mom!" Sara said. "Guess what? Carmen and I are trying out for the cheerleader squad. They have uniforms and everything!"

"That's great as long as it doesn't compete with your school work. You'll still need to keep up your grades. Plus you have church activities."

"I know, but I really, really, *really* want to make the squad," Sara pleaded.

"Well, if you really, really *really* do," Mom joked, "then I guess it's okay."

Sara squealed, jumped up, and kissed Mom on the cheek. "Thank you, thank you, thank you!"

"Laying it on a little thick, aren't you?" Alex asked.

"Leave her alone, Alex," his mom said.

Alex thought his mom looked tired tonight. Teaching a bunch of potential high school dropouts basic English couldn't be easy.

"I'll clean up the table, Mom," he said.

Mom looked shocked, and she reached over and felt his forehead.

"You feeling all right?" she teased. "I could have sworn I heard you volunteer to clean up the dishes."

"He must have fried his brains today," Sara said,

giggling.

"Nobody asked for your opinion." Alex said.

"Alex," Mom cautioned. She stood up with her plate. "Come on, I'll help you."

Alex and his mother worked quietly, clearing off the table and loading the dishwasher. As he washed the pots by hand, Mom asked, "Something on your mind?"

"Uh, huh. Just tired I guess. I've got a ton of homework for tomorrow."

"You know we haven't talked much about your dad lately. You miss him a lot?"

Alex nodded his head yes.

"It's still hard to believe he's gone," she said, "but at least I know he's in heaven."

Alex was quiet a moment before he asked, "How do you know?"

He'd thought a lot about it since Heidi started pressing him to go back to the youth group. Where was the proof? He'd prayed for his dad to get well, just like they told him to in church, but his father had still died. So what use was it? Why pray to a God who let bad stuff happen anyway?

"We might not have made church every single Sunday, but your dad had a good relationship with the Lord. Why don't you come to church with Sara and me this weekend? It might make you feel better."

"No thanks!" Alex said, draining the water out of the sink. "It's okay for you and Sara, but I don't want any part of it. Besides, I've got a lot of stuff going on."

His mother looked sad, but she didn't push him.

That night Alex laid awake thinking about his Dad and crying some into his pillow. If God couldn't save his Dad's life, how was Alex supposed to believe there was really a heaven and a hell? Maybe it was just over when you died. And if there was a heaven, how could he be sure if his dad was there? If Dad wasn't playing football somewhere good, Alex didn't want to go there either! Still angry at God, Alex fell into a restless sleep.

The next morning at school, Alex felt like he hardly took a breath until the call-backs were posted outside Coach's door. He pushed through the crowd to look at the typed list. He'd made it! So had Jeff. And so had Matt. Three seventh-graders who all wanted to be quarterbacks. Plus Chuck who wanted to be a guard.

After school, Coach Rodriguez and Coach Benson split the boys up into teams for a scrimmage. Alex was on the blue team with Chuck, Matt, an eighth-grader named Sam Johnson, and a few other guys Alex didn't know. Sam quickly took control of the team.

"Okay, Alex, you're the center," Sam said. "Matt,

why don't you QB for us? Chuck, you be wide receiver. I'll be the running back. Got it?" Then Sam pointed at the remaining eighth graders. "Now you two, we need serious tight ends. Don't let anyone through."

Alex glanced at Matt, who looked thrilled. Alex saw him take several deep breaths, trying to calm down, and heard a wheezing sound. "You okay?" Alex asked.

"Yeah, my asthma is acting up a little. It's probably just nerves." Alex watched Matt pat his pocket, checking that his inhaler was there.

The play began. Alex hiked the ball to Matt, who caught it. Immediately, Sam and another eighth grader, Benjamin, pulled back to guard him as he scanned the field to find Chuck or Rob beyond the other team's guards. Matt spotted his man and launched the ball. It sailed over the heads of the other players and into the hands of Chuck. Chuck turned and ran the ball into the end zone.

They regrouped. "Great job, Matt," Sam said. "Okay, Alex, let's see what you've got. You play quarterback this time."

Benjamin hiked Alex the ball while the other guys took off running. Alex saw that Chuck was once again wide open and signaling for Alex to throw. Alex drew his arm back to release the ball, and then remembered that Coach had criticized his distance. He couldn't risk it. Not now. He tucked the ball under his arm and ran for the end zone. He didn't make it five yards before he was tackled by a burly eighth grader.

"What was that about?" Sam asked when Alex stood up.

Alex didn't know what to say. "I'm sorry. I just panicked."

"You didn't panic," Chuck said. "You wanted to make the score yourself."

It wasn't true, but Alex knew Chuck had good reason to think it was. "Whatever," Alex said, and walked away.

After a few more plays, the scrimmage was over. "Results will be posted first thing Monday morning," Coach said. "Thanks for all your effort."

Alex knew he hadn't done as well as he could, but he thought he'd played as good as or better than Jeff and Matt. So he still had a chance.

Now he just had to wait for Monday.

Never in his life had Alex wished so much to destroy his little sister as he did that weekend. His nerves were on edge, anyway. And Sara knew it. She'd made the cheerleading team and already had her uniform. On Saturday morning, she put it on and ran around the family room practicing cheers.

"Give me an A!" she yelled.

"A," Alex said. He was lying on the sofa in his navy blue sweatpants, watching cartoons. A half-eaten bowl of Cheerios sat on the coffee table.

"Give me an L!"

"L."

"Give me an E!"

"E."

"Give me an X!"

"X."

"What's that spell?" she asked in her perkiest cheerleader voice.

"Alex, you moron," Alex said, throwing a sofa pillow at her.

"No! LOSER!" she said, and ran away giggling.

After Mom came downstairs and heard a few more of Sara's cheers, she gave her daughter strict orders to lay off.

Later that afternoon, since he and Jeff weren't on speaking terms, Alex worked at the kitchen table on his homework, answering the questions at the end of the first chapter of his social studies text. He looked up as Sara pranced into the room, tossing something up and down in her hand.

"What's that?" he asked.

"Dad's coin. Mom said I could have it," Sara said.

"*What* coin?" Alex demanded.

"Oh, the one the zebra-striped guy had at the game," she said.

"The one from the coin toss? That should be *mine*. Dad would have wanted me to have it!" Alex yelled.

"That's just too bad for you then, isn't it," Sara said. She ran up the stairs and into her room, slamming the door before Alex could catch her.

Late Saturday afternoon, Sara was finally out of his hair when the Rodriguez family picked her up to spend the night with Carmen. Alex was glad to have her out of the house, but worried about what she might say to Coach Rodriguez.

On Sunday afternoon after church, Sara invaded his room without knocking.

"Didn't Mom ever teach you how to knock, moron?" Alex said.

Sara ignored his question and asked one of her own. "Wanna know what Coach Rodriguez said about you?"

He ignored her, hoping she'd leave on her own.

"He said, 'Alex is the best kicker I've ever seen,'" she said.

Alex hated to believe her, but he had to know more. "Really?"

"Definitely," she said. "Wait, no. Maybe he said best *picker*. That's it. He said he'd never seen anyone get boogers out as well as you can."

"Get *out*!" Alex yelled, jumping off his bed and slamming the door. He heard her laughing all the way down the hall.

On Monday morning Alex woke up before his alarm went off and hurriedly dressed, arriving at school a half hour early. There was already a small crowd waiting outside the coach's office, but no lights were on inside.

"Where's Coach?" Alex asked Chuck.

"Right here," Coach said, coming up behind them. "You guys here selling Girl Scout cookies or something?"

A few guys laughed nervously.

"Oh, yeah," Coach said. "The roster. Hang on. I'll put it right up." Coach pulled a sheet out of his satchel and pinned it to the bulletin board outside his office. Then he unlocked the office door. "I wish I could take all of you on the team, but the school just can't afford it. Plus we'd have to tie a few of you on the top of the bus for road trips. But you all did a great job during tryouts. If anyone has any questions," he said, turning on his office light, "let me know." Then he closed his door.

Everyone shoved and crowded around the sheet, murmuring. By this time there were so many of them that it was hard to get a good look. Alex kept getting bumped out of the way. Chuck and Jeff were closer than he was. He saw them both scan the list, drop their heads, and back away. Alex felt bad for them, but knew that meant he had an even better shot. *If any seventh grader made it*, he thought, *it had to be me.*

Finally he pushed close enough to read the list. He looked toward the bottom for his last name. Nothing. So he checked it alphabetically by first name. Nothing there either. He frantically scanned the whole list. His name just *had* to be on the list.

Alex realized Jeff was standing beside him. "I guess this is the first year in a long time Coach hasn't taken any seventh graders," Alex said.

"What are you talking about?" Jeff asked. "Didn't you read the list?"

"I thought so," Alex said. "I'm not on there, you're not on there. Chuck's not on there—"

"Alex!" Jeff interrupted. "Matt made the team."

Alex exploded in anger. "What?! Matt made the team? Is Coach insane? Matt's gonna get *killed* out there. I'm ten times better than he is. Jeff, *you're* ten times better than he is!"

"Alex, just shut up," Jeff said, and walked away.

Alex was in total shock. How could this have happened? He wasn't on the team, but tall, gangly Matt Goodman was? Alex looked again at the list. Yep, there it was. Matt Goodman, backup QB.

A bell rang, signaling that classes would begin in ten minutes. Alex looked through the glass into Coach Rodriguez's office and saw he was alone. He wasn't sure he had time to talk to Coach and still make it to his first class, but he had to give it a shot.

"Excuse me, Coach?" Alex said, sticking his head in the door.

"Come in, Alex," Coach said. "What's up?"

Alex didn't know how to start. "I just wanted to ask you about the roster," he said finally.

"You mean, you want to know why you didn't make the team."

"Well...yeah," Alex answered, almost relieved that the coach had been so blunt.

"Alex, you're a good player. You really are. But you know how few seventh graders ever make the team. I want to give the older boys as much playing time as I can before they head for high school."

"Yeah, I know," Alex said. "But—"

"But, what, Alex?"

The words burst out of Alex. "You took Matt Goodman!"

"Is that it?" Coach asked. "Matt really impressed me at camp and during tryouts. He's a hard worker. I saw that right away. But he also takes coaching really well. He's got a good throwing arm, and if he keeps improving, he'll be as good as any on the team. And he has one of the finest attitudes I've ever seen."

Alex remembered that he hadn't always shown that he was a "team player" during tryouts. But how was he supposed to show Coach how good he was if he was always looking out for other people?

Then Alex thought about his dad. His dad would have been so disappointed in him. When his dad was in hospice, he and Alex had gone over plays and talked about the next year when Alex would be playing on the Eisenhower Middle School football team. Now he wouldn't be!

Alex hated all the sympathy and special treatment he'd gotten because of his dad's death. He just wanted to be normal. He'd resisted many of his teachers' attempts to let him out of assignments, even when his dad was really sick. He hated pity. It made him feel weak. But he was desperate. He didn't know what he'd do if he didn't get to play football that fall.

"Coach," Alex said.

"Yes, Alex," Coach answered.

"I don't know how to say this. But I'd really appreciate it if you'd reconsider letting me on the team. My dad really wanted me to play this year. I hate to let him down—keep his dreams from coming true." By sheer will, Alex squeezed out a tear and brushed it away.

Coach's eyes flashed. He had an expression on his face Alex had never seen before on the big man. Coach rose out of his chair and spoke sternly.

"Frank Rogers was a fine man and a friend of mine, Alex. I know he'd be disappointed that you didn't make the team. Don't think that didn't cross my mind when I made my decision. But he'd be even more disappointed in his son for trading on sympathy at his death just to get a slot on a football team."

Real, hot tears sprang to Alex's eyes now. Tears of shame. But he kept them from falling. He realized that even worse than losing a spot on the team was losing Coach Rodriguez's respect.

Alex started to speak, but Coach interrupted him. "Don't say anything right now, Alex. I'm too angry and disappointed in you to hear an apology right now. But if you really want to be a part of this team, you still can. I have two trainer positions and one manager position open. Think about it, Alex." The bell rang again, signaling the beginning of first period. "Now get to class."

CHAPTER:04

Alex turned and left Coach's office almost at a dead run. His mind was reeling, but he knew he had to get to history class in a hurry. He rushed around the corner toward his locker and ran into Heidi, knocking a stack of papers out of her arms. They scattered all over the gray vinyl floor. Reluctantly, knowing he'd never explain the tardy now, Alex knelt and helped her pick them up.

"Where you flying to, Superman?" she asked.

"I'm late for class. Aren't you?"

"No, I'm a teacher's aide for Mrs. Kerwin this hour. She asked me to post some flyers about tryouts for the school play. But you posted them for me—all over the floor," she said with a smile.

As he scooped up the scattered flyers, Alex mumbled, "I've really got to get to class"

"I'd hate to contribute any further to your tardiness," she said. "But since you're late already—"

"What?!" Why couldn't she just leave him alone? Especially right now? All he could think about was Coach Rodriguez and what he'd said. And now he'd get a royal chewing out by Mrs. Taylor. She hated when people were tardy.

"The youth group is going paintballing this Saturday in Broken Arrow. I thought you might like to join us. There should be fifty or sixty of us going."

"Why would I wanna go paintballing with your youth group?" he asked rudely.

"You're a guy, aren't you? Guys like to shoot things, don't they? Wait, I forgot. You probably have football practice or something."

Alex knew she wasn't being sarcastic. She just hadn't seen the team roster yet. But her confidence in him was more than he could handle.

"As it happens, I *don't* have football practice. I didn't make the team! But the last place I want to be is with some stupid bunch of Christians doing stupid paintball!" he said. "See ya."

Alex took off running down the hall and slid around another corner to Mrs. Taylor's history class. His four-foot-nine teacher could look six feet tall when she wanted to make a point. She stopped lecturing and looked over at Alex as he quietly opened and shut the door.

"You're late," she said. Alex didn't think it was

necessary for her to state the obvious. "Where's your permission slip?"

Alex nervously shifted his weight from one sneaker to another, as his buddies in the back of the class snickered.

"Do you have a reason for being tardy?" she said sternly.

"I was talking to Coach Rodriguez."

The fifty-something, gray-haired teacher sniffed her disapproval. "About football, I suppose."

Alex edged toward his seat on the aisle and sat down. "Yes ma'am."

"Don't get comfortable, Mr. Rogers," she said, tapping her marker on the whiteboard. You'll need a permission slip from Principal Docking before you're allowed back in my class, and I'll expect you to attend detention this afternoon."

Not knowing what to say, Alex just sat there.

"NOW, Mr. Rogers!"

"Yes, ma'am."

Alex fled Mrs. Taylor's history class like a rabbit being shot at, but once he was in the hallway, he slowed down and walked to Principal Docking's office. No sense rushing to punishment. Plus he wasn't that crazy about studying ancient civilizations, and the longer he took, the less of Mrs. Taylor's lecture he'd have to listen to."

As he walked into the office, the school secretary Mrs. Patchett looked over her reading glasses at him.

"Whatcha need, Alex? A tardy slip?"

"I was talking to Coach Rodriguez and was late to Mrs. Taylor's class. She sent me to see Mr. Docking."

The secretary smiled kindly. "He's in a meeting right now. Why don't I sign a permissions slip and you can go back to class."

"Great!"

Mrs. Patchett scribbled on a pink slip of paper and signed the principal's name followed by her initials. "This will get you in today. But no more tardies!"

"No, ma'am! Thanks, Mrs. Patchett!"

Alex felt like he'd dodged that bullet. He'd heard stories about Mr. Docking and how strict he was. He didn't want to go there . . . ever.

Before returning to history class, Alex stopped by his locker to pick up his math textbook. That way he could finish up the last two problems he couldn't get last night before class began.

Alex quickly spun his combination and opened the upper locker door. A small folded-up piece of notebook paper fell out of his locker on the floor. Somebody must have wedged it in the door. Before reading it, he glanced at the picture taped to the inside of the door. It was of him and his dad at the

Tulsa zoo. Dad would be so disappointed in him if he knew what he'd done in Coach's office. Quickly, he pushed the thought from his mind and read the hastily scribbled note:

"Alex, I'm really sorry you didn't make the team. And I'm sorry for making you late to class. The paintball invitation still stands. Your Stupid Christian Friend, Heidi."

Ah man! Why couldn't Heidi just leave him alone? He wadded up the note and stuffed it into his front pocket. Paintball was cool, but he didn't want people thinking he and Heidi were hanging out together.

Sighing, Alex slammed his locker door and headed back to Mrs. Taylor's class.

Alex opened the back door as quietly as he could. He was hoping he could sneak up to his room without running into his mom or Sara. He just wanted to be alone for awhile and think. It was starting to really sink in. He wasn't on the football team. Not only that, but he'd made Coach Rodriguez angry, probably ruining his chance of getting on the team next year as well. He'd let down his dad after all.

Usually his mom stayed late at school and he got home at least an hour before she did. But as he walked through the living room toward the staircase, he heard his mom ask, "How was your day, Alex?"

Alex didn't know if she'd heard about the team roster. "Fine," he said, hoping not to talk about it right then. He kept walking.

"Really?" she said. "You're not disappointed about not making the team?"

"How did you find out?"

"I asked," she said. "I know it was really important to you."

"It's no big deal. He hardly ever puts seventh graders on the team," Alex said, hoping he sounded convincing.

"I admire you for taking it so well," she said. "Since you seem to be in such a good mood, I have a favor to ask of you."

Uh-oh. His mom's "favors" usually involved chasing after garden snakes, or watching Sara, which was pretty much the same thing.

"I've got a conference this Saturday, and I was hoping you could watch Sara," she said.

Alex thought fast. "Sorry, Mom, I can't. I'm going to play paintball with the youth group."

"You'd rather play paintball than help out your dear old mom?" she asked with a smile.

"Heidi Hendricks asked me to go this morning. It's a church thing."

"Oh, really? I thought you weren't interested in church activities lately," his mom said.

Alex shrugged. "Thought I'd give it another shot," he said. "Otherwise I'd be glad to watch Sara."

At that, his mother laughed. "Don't lie to your mother, Alex. But don't worry, you can go. I'll see if Sara can spend the day at the Rodriguez's."

Alex went up to his room, glad that Heidi had invited him to something. He actually loved playing paintball. Even if it was with Heidi and the youth group, it would be way better than taking care of Sara.

Alex wasn't nearly as eager to get to school on Tuesday as he was on Monday. But he also couldn't afford another tardy. So he was at his locker well before the warning bell. He was first in his seat at homeroom, but the rest of his morning classes were a blur. All he could think about was not making the team.

At lunch, he picked up a tray and joined the long line, scanning the cafeteria for where everyone was sitting. When he paid for his lunch, he looked over at the football table. Last week he thought he'd be sitting there. Now he watched as Matt took his tray over and sat down beside Sam Johnson, who patted the newcomer on the shoulder.

As Alex looked longingly at the coveted spot in the lunch room, he finally noticed someone standing beside him. It was Jeff.

"Hey," Jeff said.

"Hey." Alex knew Jeff was waiting for an apology,

but Alex wasn't very good at apologizing. Still, he took a stab at it. "Jeff, look, I'm sorry I was such a jerk. I really wanted to be on the team. I still do. But I don't want that to . . ." Alex's voice trailed off.

"I know it's hard, man," Jeff said. "But you knew making the team was a long shot for all of us."

"Yeah," said Alex. "I know." The problem was he'd never admitted that to himself before. "I just want you to know . . . thanks for being my friend."

"No problem."

Just then, Chuck walked up, and the three rejected seventh graders all strolled toward the table where they normally sat.

As they took their seats, Craig Hashimoto yelled, "Hey Jeff, Chuck! Come on over and sit with us!"

Jeff glanced at Alex. It was obvious he felt uncomfortable. "Thanks, Craig. Maybe tomorrow!" Jeff said.

Chuck looked ready to abandon them both for the football team but followed Jeff's lead instead.

Everything was quiet at the table for a minute. Then Alex finally asked, "What's going on?"

"Chuck and I told Coach we'd work as trainers for the football team," Jeff said. "We go to our first practice today."

"What's the point?" Alex asked. "You'll just be glorified water boys. Why waste your time?"

"I guess it wouldn't do any good to ask if you'd like to be manager," Jeff said.

"Forget it, Jeff," Chuck said. "He thinks he's too good for any of that. Excuse me." He took his tray and left.

"What's his problem?" Alex asked.

"I don't think he appreciated the 'water boy' comment. Neither did I," Jeff said.

"Aw, come on, you know what I mean."

"Yeah, I do," Jeff said. "I used to think the same thing. But I talked to Coach yesterday, and there's really a lot more to it. I'm actually looking forward to it."

"I'm really glad for you," Alex said, meaning it. "But it's just not for me. Not right now."

"No sweat," Jeff said. "Subject closed."

That afternoon, Alex remembered he needed to talk to Heidi about the youth group trip. He finally found her in the hallway outside the science lab.

"Hey," he said, trying to sound casual, "if it's not too late, I'd like to go to that paintball thing."

She looked a little surprised, but tried not to sound it. "No, not too late at all. I'll be at church tomorrow night. I'll bring you a permission slip for your mom to sign. Can you be at church by nine o'clock Saturday morning?"

"No problem," he said. "See ya then."

Alex waved and headed down the hall to his locker. Matt was waiting for him. Alex hadn't spoken to Matt since his rival made the team. He wasn't sure he wanted to now.

"Hey," Alex said. "Congratulations, I guess."

"Look, Alex," Matt said. "I can understand if you're mad. I think you should have made the team. Or Jeff. Or Chuck. Anybody but me."

"You sound like you don't even want to be on the team!" Alex said, feeling a little angry.

"Yes, I do. I just feel in over my head. I don't know how I'm ever going to learn all the plays."

Alex started to feel a little sorry for him. He could tell Matt was worried. "You'll be fine," Alex said.

"You're so good at all that stuff, man. You always know the plays, the strategies—"

"What's your point?" Alex asked.

"Nothing, it's just that—"

"It's just that you're on the team and I'm not," Alex said. He slammed his locker closed and walked away. If Matt thought Alex was going to help him, he must have already taken too many hits to the head.

On Saturday morning, Alex's mom dropped him off in the church parking lot on the way to her conference. As he got out of the car, Alex started to feel nervous. He hadn't been to church since his dad's memorial service. And he certainly hadn't gone out of his way to be nice to the kids from church. For the first time ever he was anxious to see Heidi. There she was, waiting for him, but instead of her red hair all wild around her face, it hung down her back in a French braid.

"Hey, Alex! I'm glad you made it," she said.

"Afraid I wouldn't show up?" Alex smiled.

"Not me. I'm fearless," she said. "Come with me. We're on the red bus."

The bus wasn't actually red, but it did have a piece of red construction paper taped to the inside of the front windshield. It looked like there were about twenty-five kids on board, and Alex slid in next to Heidi near the back. The blue bus looked just as full. Both the junior and senior high youth groups must have turned out to play paintball.

Heidi was unusually quiet. "What's up with the silent treatment?" Alex asked.

"Sorry, I'm just a little nervous."

"About what?" he asked. "Sitting next to me?"

"About paintball. I've never done this before."

"I thought you were fearless!" Alex said.

"Only in regard to you, Mr. Rogers," Heidi said. "When it comes to being shot with hard paint pellets, I'm as chicken as the next kid."

"You'll be fine, Heidi," Alex assured her. "Just

keep your helmet on and don't lift your face shield."

At the front of the bus Geri, the pretty twenty-something youth leader, stood up.

"I'm glad you could all make it," she said, raising her voice over the noise. "Please pass up your permission slips. Guess I should have gotten those before I let you on the bus, huh? Here are the ground rules. Each one of you needs a partner. I know the buddy system seems a bit childish, but it helps me keep track of everyone."

"Will you be my buddy?" Heidi asked.

"No, but I'll be your neighbor," Alex said.

"You know," she said, "I've been dying to make a Mr. Rogers joke about you, but I thought you might be sick of them."

"Yeah, I've pretty much heard them all."

"So I guess you don't wear many cardigan sweaters," said Raf's voice behind them. Alex hadn't even seen him get on the bus.

Alex looked over his shoulder, grinning. "I do have a stoplight in my living room though."

Raf laughed. "I've gotta admit I'm surprised to see you here, Dude."

"I'm a little surprised to be here myself," Alex said.

Sitting next to Raf was a pretty African-American girl with her hair French-braided just like Heidi's. Alex thought it was smart. They were going to be running through a lot of brush.

"This is my girlfriend, Keisha," Raf said.

"Hi, Keisha."

"Hey." Keisha's grin came easily, as if she spent a lot of time laughing.

"Keisha was on the trip to Mexico I told you about," Heidi said. "She's a workin' fool! You should have seen her carry lumber. Keisha about worked the guys under the table."

"Hey!" Raf said, laughing. "We were on the same team down there. It took all of us to build that house." Keisha punched him in the arm, and the two grinned at each other.

"I figured if I walked fast, the bugs couldn't eat me up," Keisha said. "Those mosquitoes could have carried off a small child."

"Remember the outhouse?" Heidi asked. She shivered.

"Yes, I remember that outhouse," Keisha said, "and that giant black snake."

Raf guffawed. "She came running out of that place screaming like a banshee."

"You'll have to come with us next time, Alex," said Keisha. "We had a ball, plus we did some good things for Christ."

"Yeah, maybe I will," Alex said.

The four of them talked the whole way to Broken

Arrow, and Alex heard a lot more stories about different missions trips Keisha had been on. He could have listened to her all day.

Before they knew it, the buses were pulling into the Triple-R Game Ranch.

"Okay, people," Geri said, when their bus had stopped. "Here's the plan. Go to the locker rooms and change into your paintball clothes. Then meet me in the lobby to get your equipment."

Alex had gone paintballing with his older cousins from Muskogee several times, so he knew how to dress. It was a warm September day, but Alex had brought an old mechanic's jumpsuit of his grandfather's, as well as a padded collar for his neck. Kneepads, an old pair of BMX racing gloves, and a real military-style ammunition belt with small pouches and hook holders completed his uniform.

When Alex emerged from the locker room, everyone turned to gape at him. A few of them started to snicker. Raf laughed good-naturedly.

"Laugh it up," Alex said. "But you'll see. I'll be the one laughing later!"

Heidi met Alex outside the locker rooms. She had changed from her shorts and T-shirt into long pants and a long-sleeved jersey. She looked at Alex and burst out laughing.

"I'm sorry," she said, between giggles. "I'm not

laughing *at* you." Then she bent over, giggling and snorting, helpless with laughter.

"Now I *know* you've never done this before," Alex said. "Hey, didn't you have a T-shirt on?"

"Yeah, why?" Heidi asked.

"Go get it and bring it here," Alex told her.

Heidi soon came back out with her T-shirt. Alex rolled it up and tied it loosely around her neck so that the thickest part was at the back.

"The helmets are great for your head, but those paintballs sting like crazy when you get hit on the back of your neck," Alex told her.

Together, they headed for the lobby where Geri waited for her group.

"Alex, Heidi, you're on my team," Geri said. "You get the pink paintballs."

Heidi went to the counter and got her gun, CO_2 canister, and asked for a box of a hundred pink paintballs. She was then fitted with a helmet that had a heavy face shield.

Alex got four hundred pink paintballs. He was then fitted with his helmet.

"That's all you got?" Alex asked when he saw Heidi's box.

"Yeah, why?" Heidi replied in confusion. "Isn't that enough?"

"If you hold the trigger in, the CO_2 can shoot

out ten paintballs before you even realize it," he explained. "Take some of mine."

Alex reached into his bag and handed her one of his boxes of a hundred paintballs. Then he showed her how to load the gun.

"When we get out in the field, watch your back," Alex said. "You wanna always be looking around, making sure you're not being ambushed. And try to stay low and hidden. Keep your shirt tucked in so you don't get snagged on any bushes or tree branches."

"You're really good at this," Heidi said.

"Good at what? Paintball?" he asked.

"Probably. I haven't seen you on the field yet. I meant, you're really good at explaining stuff. You should be a teacher or a coach or something."

"Thanks," Alex said, but he didn't want to teach or coach. He wanted to *play*. This was gonna be fun!

CHAPTER:05

After the entire group had suited up, they looked like a rag-tag army. Some wore camouflage-green shirts or pants, and those who were inexperienced dressed in jeans and T-shirts. *Boy, are they gonna get creamed,* Alex thought.

Geri called them all together for some brief instruction by one of the field supervisors.

"There's one flag out in a clearing in the middle of the woods," he said. "The object of the game is to make it from the start in an open field into a wooded area and into the clearing where the flag hangs from a pole. The team that captures the flag wins. Pretty simple."

After he finished speaking, Geri divided the group into four teams, with twelve players each. Geri would lead one team, with the other three being led by Raf Rodriguez, Tom Kirk, and Mia Chen—all seniors.

Alex and Heidi's group were given two-inch pink armbands to wear, and the other groups wore similar orange, green, or blue armbands.

Alex secretly wished he'd been made a leader, but he knew it was stupid to be disappointed. He wasn't old enough and no one even knew if he could play paintball. But still, he just hoped Geri knew what she was doing.

The teams were sent to four separate starting points surrounding the wooded area. Each team was provided a map of the ranch and given fifteen minutes after the sound of the first horn to plan their strategy.

At the first horn, Geri told her team to sit in a huddle and laid the course map on the ground.

"We're here," she said, pointing to a spot on the map. Alex and the others leaned over to get a good view of their present position. "And this is our objective. This path will lead us to the flag."

"How come we're taking such a roundabout way," Heidi asked.

"The other squads will assume we've taken the quicker route, and that will be their downfall," Geri said. "We'll head into a thicker part of the woods and scope out the flag. Everyone with me?"

"Yeah!" everyone chorused. Alex had to admit it was a good plan.

"Why don't we leave two players at the base of the hill so the other teams think we're still coming?" Alex suggested.

"Great idea!" said Geri. "Any volunteers?"

"I'll do it," a girl named Darlene said.

"Me too," her friend Sherry quickly agreed.

"Great!" Geri said. "When we get to the bottom of the hill, you two drop into the tall grass and wait. You'll definitely come under fire from the other teams. But if you can hold out and dodge their shots, wait until one of us flags you at the trail or you see downed players walking out. Then we'll spot you as you run for the path."

Geri led the way, and the squad ran down the hill into the open field. As the group jogged down the path, Geri pointed to the tall grassy area, which she wanted Darlene and Sherry to stake out. The two girls dropped into position and prepared their guns.

Geri's squad, now numbering ten, ran across the wide-open trampled field and entered the wooded center just as the second horn sounded. Kicking through piles of leaves, they scattered away from the path into the camouflaged safety of the trees.

As they ran, Geri pointed to where each pair should stop and guard. As the squad narrowed down to four, She pointed to a spot for Alex and Heidi.

They took their positions on the ground and watched as their leader and her "buddy," a sophomore named Alan that neither of them knew, made their way to the edge of the center clearing. A moment later, the air horns sounded. Alex and Heidi hugged the ground, listening to players running through thick underbrush and paintballs splatting when players were hit. Adrenaline raced through Alex's veins. He was pumped!

The two crawled to nearby trees and sat on the ground facing the direction of the center field. They had a clear line of sight from opposite sides of the path. They waited for other players to run past so they could fire on them from behind.

Suddenly, a lone scout, sporting an orange armband, ran by. Heidi prepared to fire but Alex motioned for her to hold. Heidi nodded agreement. Just then, four more of the orange team ran by.

He pointed to the last two enemy players, and Heidi aimed. On Alex's signal, they both fired, shooting the same runner in the back. He stopped in his tracks and dropped to his knees, holding up both hands.

But the sounds of gunfire had alerted the other runner, who turned and rapidly scanned the thick woods for his would-be assailants. Before he could spot their location, Heidi and Alex let loose with repeated shots to his chest. He also dropped to the ground. The two forward orange players broke into a run. Alex and Heidi were safe for the moment.

Alex carefully peeked around the tree to see if he could spy other players running toward them. None were in sight. He signaled for Heidi to rise. The two met in the center path and stood back-to-back. Working together, they walked forward on the path: Heidi face forward and Alex facing the rear.

"How did you know?" Heidi whispered.

"Know what?" Alex whispered back.

"About the other orange players coming?"

"Razor-sharp instinct," Alex said and smiled.

A few minutes later, Alex and Heidi met up with four other teammates. The group moved forward until they heard footsteps. Then they dispersed into the underbrush and knelt down. The path was soon overrun with six players sporting blue armbands.

The blue team scanned the woods but lost two players before even knowing what hit them. Like lightning, the entire pink team opened fire, downing the rest of the blue group. Unfortunately, two pink players were also shot.

Checking Heidi for any hits, he whispered, "You're okay. Let's go!"

Alex and Heidi regrouped with the other two surviving pink players. With the clearing in sight, they ran toward the rendezvous point. Hearing what sounded like a bird calling, they all turned toward a giant, overturned stump. It was easily six feet around and shielded Geri and Alan, along with four other teammates.

When Geri saw two more of her squadron still standing, she gave the thumbs-up sign. Signaling two players to spot her, she pulled out the map and began speaking through her face shield.

"Okay, I need two volunteers to potentially sacrifice themselves. You'll have to circle round and charge out of the woods into the open, but wait until you're far enough away from us to distract the others."

Alex looked at Heidi, who nodded her approval.

"We'll do it," said Alex.

"Great," Geri said. "Be careful but stay visible as much as possible. It should draw out the other teams. Once you two are shot down, two more will go. The last two will head straight for the flag."

Alex and Heidi separated and made their way around the perimeter before jumping out into the grassy field to face their doom. Within seconds, airburst shots seemed to come from all directions.

Suddenly, at least a dozen players ran out into the open, some firing at the pink decoys and some firing on the other now-revealed shooters of other teams. Alex looked over to see Heidi get hit in the arm. She immediately dropped to her knees and raised her arms into the air.

Through his face mask, Alex saw a member of the green team charging the flag. He turned to signal his team and took a hit in his back. He was supposed to drop to his knees. But because he hesitated, another shot hit him square in the chest. Despite all his padding, the stinging was fierce. He dropped to his knees and raised his hands.

Players were dropping all around him as paintball shots hit their marks. That's when another group of two pink players ran into the field to scout and block, drawing fire. Right behind them, Geri, followed by Alan, charged out of the woods and straight for the flag. As they approached, Geri turned toward the enemy players to block Alan, who ran toward the flagpole. Geri covered her soldier well.

A small group of surviving green players came rushing out of the woods on the path the pink team had been guarding. But as they ran towards Alan, they too were downed. Darlene and Sherry, the two pink players who had been in hiding all this time, came running down the beaten path and out into the clearing to save the day. Geri, hit in the back of her helmet, had no choice but to drop to her knees and raise her hands.

Now it was all up to Alan. Alex watched as Alan dodged toward the flag tower and began to unfasten the rope that held it aloft. Alan lowered the flag and as he did, a horn sounded, declaring the end of the match.

"Game over! The winner is the Pink Team!" announced a voice over the loudspeaker.

The downed players rose and surrounded Alan. Everyone congratulated him, even the losing teams.

"I don't think I've ever won anything before!" Alan said, laughing and holding up the flag.

Alex felt really good. He didn't care that he wasn't the one holding the flag. It just felt good to be part of the winning team. And he realized that if he hadn't suggested that Darlene and Sherry stay behind, they might not have won.

"I think my gun is jammed," Sherry said when they regrouped.

"Let me see it," Alex offered. Confidently taking it apart, he soon had it working again. They were able to play three more matches that day, and Alex became the "fix it" guy, helping everyone with gear and ammo loading. Several times, Geri asked Alex for strategic advice.

When Alex, Heidi, and the others wearily pulled themselves back on the red bus for home, they were sore and exhausted.

"You were right," Raf said, rubbing his neck. "I'm not laughing at your outfit now, Alex. Next time, I'll be better dressed. You'll be calling me Mr. Paintball."

Keisha punched Raf's shoulder, unsympathetically. "You'll live, big guy."

"I thought you were supposed to take my side," Raf said.

"This is just getting you in shape for football."
Keisha said, laughing. "Man, that was fun, but I feel
like somebody threw me in a dryer with a bunch of
tennis balls."

They all laughed.

The rest of the ride home was pretty quiet.
Everyone was too worn out to talk much. Alex adjust-
ed an ice bag for Heidi, who had suffered a shot to
the arm. "Thanks," she said. A huge welt was already
turning black and blue.

As people around him started to doze off, Alex
thought about the day. He'd had a great time, even
when they hadn't won. He enjoyed playing, but he
realized he'd enjoyed helping the other players too.

The blazing red and orange sun was sinking on
the horizon when the bus pulled into the church
parking lot, where parents waited in cars. Most of the
kids were only thinking about getting off the buses as
fast as possible and going home to climb into bed.

"Don't sleep too late!" Geri instructed. "We've
got church in the morning!"

Everyone groaned. Alex was relieved he didn't
have to set the alarm for church, but then he felt
kind of sad. Suddenly, he realized he might not get
to hang out with most of these people again.

As if reading his thoughts, Heidi said, "There's
another movie night next Saturday in the church

gym. Wanna come?"

"I'll think about it," Alex said. But he knew there wasn't much that would keep him away.

That night, Alex slept hard. When he rolled over to look at his clock the next morning, it was already 10:30. He wondered if Raf and Heidi were already at church. For the first time in a long time, he almost wished he were there too.

Alex's feelings about God were really complicated. He prayed a lot when his dad first got sick. And when the Rogers managed to make it to church, people would come up to Alex and tell him they were praying for his dad. Alex just figured with all that praying, his dad had to get better. When he didn't, Alex stopped trusting God. He even felt angry toward the people at his church. How could they go on singing songs about a God who had let his dad die?

But Alex couldn't convince himself that God didn't exist. It's just that they weren't on speaking terms. Deep down, Alex did believe in heaven. And he hoped his dad was there.

So when Heidi first started asking him to come back to church, he wasn't the least bit interested. He had thought Heidi and the rest of her Christian friends were a bunch of psychos. But there was nothing weird about Raf Rodriguez, and *he* seemed pretty much into the God thing.

As he got to know Heidi better, he realized she wasn't so strange, either. Or at least, she was strange in a good way. She was always nice to him and to others. And she could be really fun to be around. They had a great time as paintball partners.

Lying in bed that Sunday morning, Alex felt really confused. He wasn't ready to let God back into his life, but he wasn't ready to shut Raf and Heidi out, either.

On top of the God thing, he was really confused about the football team. At first he thought he'd never agree to be the team manager. But after yesterday, he wasn't so sure. He loved playing and the competition, but he also really enjoyed helping other people play better. Maybe showing Heidi how to load her paintball gun wasn't so different from taping up an injured player's fingers, or running the stat sheets to Coach.

CHAPTER:06

On Monday morning Alex and Jeff walked to school together, something they hadn't done for awhile. They were quiet at first. Alex finally broke the silence.

"How's football practice?" Alex asked.

Jeff looked hesitant.

"It's okay," Alex said. "I really want to know."

"It's going great! Chuck and I are in charge of running water bottles and towels out to the players on the bench. Then at the end of the game, we check in their dirty uniforms to send out to a laundry."

"Keeps you busy," Alex said.

"Yeah. The best part though is getting to work right next to Coach Rodriguez. I've learned a ton of stuff about the game just from watching him."

Alex looked over at Jeff and noticed how happy he seemed just to be part of the team, even if he didn't play. Soon, they were pushing their way through the crowd of students streaming in the front door.

"Hey," Alex said, "I'll see ya in class. I've got something important I need to do."

"Sure, later."

Jeff sauntered down the hall toward his locker, while Alex took long, purposeful strides toward Coach Rodriquez's office. Remembering the last conversation he'd had with Coach made Alex feel a little sick inside. He'd been a total jerk. He just hoped Coach would still give him a shot.

Alex rapped on the open doorway.

"Come in," Coach Rodriguez said, looking up from his desk.

"Morning, Coach," Alex said. He hesitated and then took a deep breath and dove in. "I wanted to come by and tell you how sorry I am about what happened the other day." Embarrassed, he found it hard to look Coach in the eye.

"I hope I wasn't too hard on you, Alex," Coach Rodriguez said. "Apology accepted. You have a lot going for you, so I really hated it when you tried to manipulate me. Your dad was a great guy, and I know he would expect you to earn a place on the team."

"I know," Alex said. "I'm really sorry." Then he took a deep breath. "Coach, there's just one more thing. Is that manager's position still open?"

A broad smile spread over the coach's tanned

face. "Absolutely! Can you start today?"

"Today? Yeah, sure."

"I'll see you on the field after school then," Coach said.

It had taken all of Alex's courage to ask Coach for the position. He didn't have any left over to tell Jeff and Chuck. So they were as surprised as everyone else when Alex showed up at practice.

"Welcome our new team manager, Alex Rogers," Coach said at the start of practice.

Everybody clapped, and Jeff slapped Alex on the back, grinning at him like the old days. "Cool!"

"Now let's get to work," Coach said.

Alex thought playing football was tough, but this was tougher. He ran back and fourth between the coaches, delivering messages. He kept the scorebook and stat sheets for all of the players, which required total concentration, and he had to wear a tie on game days. *A tie!* Talk about sacrifice! Every night that week, Alex went home exhausted, thinking about the upcoming first game of the season.

On Tuesday afternoon Alex made it to the locker room before the rest of the guys. Or so he thought. He heard someone muttering and went looking for the sound. He found Matt sitting in a corner, shuffling a bunch of hand-made flash cards.

"What's up, Dude?" Alex asked.

Matt looked embarrassed. "I'm trying to learn the rules. You know. Strategies. Plays. Half the time I don't know what Coach is talking about when he tells me what to do."

Suddenly, Alex remembered that Matt had tried to ask him for help before, but Alex had refused.

Alex sat down beside Matt on the cold locker room floor. "Here, let me take a look at those." Alex shuffled through the cards, reorganizing them.

"Look, this pile is offensive plays. Here's another for defensive plays. Don't try to look at them all at once. You'll just get confused. Pick a category, and stick with it until you've got it down."

"What about this one," Matt asked as he held up a unique card. Alex recognized the "corridor" from his dad's memories of college ball. He studied it for a moment before commenting.

"It's a corridor play," Alex explained. "Basically, the quarterback relies on his entire offensive line to push forward and form a corridor for the QB to run straight through. That way, the quarterback has teammates watching his rear and his front. It's a tough play, but if it can work, it's like getting an armed escort to a touchdown."

Alex thought to himself for a moment. *That's what we did at paintball the other day. When the team works together, you can do amazing things. I'm part of this team!*

"Thanks, Alex. It was really confusing until you explained it."

"Hey, if you'd like, maybe we can work on this together," Alex said.

"You'd do that?" Matt asked.

"Sure. After all, I am the team manager. How about we start during lunch tomorrow."

"You gotta deal!" Matt said.

Alex thought about football during breakfast, lunch, and dinner. Literally. In the mornings before school, he made notes about plays for Matt. During lunch, they worked together on all the stuff Matt needed to learn. And at dinner, Alex practiced his passing game in the backyard. He even worried about the team. Would number 55 ever learn to tackle? Did number 28 have the speed he needed? And most of all, would Matt blow it in the first game?

"What's *wrong* with you, Alpo?" Sara asked him during dinner Thursday night.

"Huh?"

"She's asked you to pass the potatoes three times," his mom said.

"I bet he's just dreaming about his *girlfriend*," Sara teased.

"Shut up!" Alex responded.

"Alex!" his mother warned. "What girlfriend? Oh, that nice girl Heidi from church?"

"Heidi is not my girlfriend!" Alex growled.

"Who is then?" Sara asked.

"Nobody!"

The phone rang, and Sara dove for it. "Rogers' residence, Sara speaking," she said in her sweetest voice. She never answered the phone that properly when their mother wasn't around. "Yes, he's right here. In fact, we were just talking about you."

Making no attempt to cover the phone, she yelled, "AAALEXXX, it's HEIIDDEEE!" She started giggling uncontrollably.

Thankfully, it was a cordless. Alex grabbed the phone from Sara and ran upstairs to his room. "Heidi," he said, trying to sound casual. "What's up?"

"Was that Sara?" she asked. "She sounds so grown up. She was always such a sweetheart."

"Yeah, whatever."

"I was just calling to see if you were coming to movie night on Saturday," she said. "I'm in charge of the popcorn machine, and I need some help. After witnessing your prowess on the paintball field, I feel confident you're up to the concessions challenge."

Alex could hear the smile in her voice, but he had completely forgotten about youth group. Now he wasn't sure he wanted to go. He was getting behind on his homework. And he knew Sara would never let him hear the end of it if he met Heidi at church. Oh, who cared? He wasn't going to let Sara ruin his life.

"Alex? You still there?"

"What time?" he asked.

"To help set up, six-thirty sharp."

"I'll be there."

"You can ask your friend Jeff to come, too, if you want," Heidi said.

"Uh, yeah." *Jeff!* Alex was pretty sure Jeff wouldn't be interested.

The first game on Friday night went by in a blur. Alex was so focused on keeping the scorebook accurate that the quarters flew by. Since the game was so tight, Matt stayed on the bench, which was okay with him and Alex. Alex wasn't sure his nerves could take it. When the final horn blew, Eisenhower had squeaked out a win against Union Middle School with a score of 21 to 20.

"Your day will come," Alex said to Matt. "Better to be sent in when the game's not so tight.

"Thanks for all the prep work," Matt said, looking relieved. "I'll be even better prepared next week."

Alex didn't realize it, but Coach was standing right behind him and heard his encouraging words to Matt. As they all walked off the field, Alex was in his own world, working out team strategies that could help Coach lead the team to wider-margin victories.

When Saturday afternoon rolled around, Alex started to regret that he'd agreed to go to movie night at church. He hadn't even asked his mom for a ride yet. When he came down from his room, Mom was sitting at the kitchen table, which was piled high with papers.

"School stuff?" Alex said.

"No. Actually some old papers and things of your father's. I've had all this stuff in boxes and just haven't felt like dealing with it. But it needs to be gone through."

Alex sat down beside his mom. "Look at this stuff! Is this Dad?" He held up a photo of a young man standing next to what looked like the Pope.

"That's your father at the wax museum in London. He went when he was in college. Here's another one of him with the wax Prince Charles. And another one with Gandhi." She held the pictures in her hand for a moment. "That's how we met, you know."

"I thought you met at a fraternity cook-out. Not in London," Alex said.

"We did. I was dating your father's roommate at the time. I'd gone up to his room—"

Alex raised his eyebrows.

"It's not what you're thinking. It was cold that night, and Gavin and I went up to their room so

I could borrow a sweatshirt. While I was there, I noticed this picture of your dad. I'd never met him and wanted to know what Gavin's roommate looked like. So I was looking at his desk—"

"You mean you were snooping," Alex said.

"If you want to call it that, then, I was snooping, when I found this picture of your father with Gandhi. I was pretty naïve back then. I sort of knew who Gandhi was, but I didn't know when he'd died. I thought your father had really met him. I was staring at the picture when he walked in." His mom started to chuckle. "He told me he'd met Gandhi before college when he'd worked in the Peace Corps."

"And you believed him?"

"Enough to borrow his sweatshirt instead of Gavin's," his mom said, slyly. "I soon learned that I could never be sure when your dad was teasing me." She was quiet for a moment. When she looked up, her eyes were moist with unshed tears. "So when he told me he was dying, I just couldn't believe him."

Alex took his mom's hand and squeezed it. Then she sniffed and brushed tears away.

"I'm sure you didn't come down here to listen to me talk about my college days," she said in a carefully cheerful voice. "What do you need?"

"Actually, there's this thing at church tonight. Some kind of movie or something. I was wondering if you could give me a ride," Alex said.

"Sure. What time do you need to be there?"

"Six-thirty. I'm supposed to help Heidi . . . to help pop the popcorn," he said, looking embarrassed.

"What's the sudden interest in church? I thought you told me this summer you didn't want anything to do with it."

"I'm not going to church, really. Just the building. I mean, for a movie. I've got some friends there."

"Friends?" his mom asked, a smile tickling at the side of her mouth. Alex knew she'd just love to know if there was a girl involved.

"Raf and I have been hanging out some lately," he said quickly.

"He's such a great kid," his mom said. "Well, whatever the reason, I'm glad you're going. It's been a hard year for all of us, and it's time you had a little fun. Plus we all need to rely on someone a little bigger than ourselves. We'll leave around six-fifteen."

Mom turned her attention again to the old photos and memorabilia scattered on the table. Alex figured she wanted to be alone. And he sure had plenty of homework to keep him busy before he left. He turned on his heel and took the stairs two at a time.

Heidi was waiting for him outside the church when he and his mom pulled up.

"That doesn't look like Raf," Mrs. Rogers said. "Don't worry. I won't ask. What time should I pick you up?"

"Around ten," Alex answered, and got out before she could say anything else. She waved at him as she pulled away in her old station wagon.

"I waited for you out here because the front door is still locked," Heidi said. "I was afraid you wouldn't be able to get in."

They walked around to the back of the brick building to the "family life center," which was basically a gym with some carpet. Geri was already there. So were Raf and Keisha, who were setting up the projector.

"So, what are we watching?" Alex asked.

"One of my favorites," Heidi said. "*The Princess Bride*. Have you seen it?"

"Do cows eat hay?" he answered.

"I guess that's a big *yes*! Come on. Help me figure this out," she said, pointing to the popcorn machine.

By seven o'clock, the room had filled up with kids of all ages, along with the smell of slightly burnt popcorn. The movie started, and soon everyone could be heard quoting their favorite lines.

"We watch this one a lot," Heidi whispered to Alex. "It's hard to find movies that everyone likes that don't have too much bad language or other stuff."

When the movie was over, Geri flipped the lights

on. Startled by the brightness, everybody covered their eyes and groaned.

"Turn the lights down!" someone shouted.

"Okie, dokie," Geri responded, and turned most of them back off. "If you promise to stay awake, we'll have our prayer time in the dark."

Prayer time? Alex didn't remember Heidi mentioning anything about prayer time. Geri pulled out a Bible and began reading:

"Not even a sparrow, worth only half a penny, can fall to the ground without your Father knowing it. And the very hairs on your head are all numbered. So don't be afraid; you are more valuable to him than a whole flock of sparrows."

Geri closed her Bible. "That comes from Matthew 10, verses 29 to 31. Jesus is reminding his followers how much God cares for each of them. And for each one of us. If God cares so much for the sparrows that he knows what happens to each one, and if he knows you so well that he knows how many hairs are on your head, then you can trust that he loves and cares about you. You are of great value to God."

Geri was quiet for a moment, as if she wanted her words to sink in. It was the first time Alex had heard anything out of the Bible since his father's funeral. Alex had thought a great deal about why God would allow his father to die, but he'd never thought too much about God's feelings for him—Alex. Did God really know him that well?

Geri asked if there were any prayer requests. A few kids mentioned sick grandparents. One girl said her parents might get a divorce. Something inside Alex told him to raise his hand and ask for prayer. But he quickly ignored the impulse. Why would he want anyone to pray for him?

"Okay," Geri said. "Let's pray. Dear Father God, thank you for the fun we've had tonight. Thank you for Heidi and Alex, who prepared the popcorn, and for Raf and Keisha, who got the projector set up so that I wouldn't have to try and figure it out. Many of us here tonight have shared our concerns for friends and family. Lord, you've told us to come to you with our fear and worry, so that's what we're doing. Please send your Holy Spirit to work in every situation we've talked about. We trust you to know what's best for them. Comfort and give peace to each one in this room. In Jesus' name we pray. Amen."

Soon everyone was standing, stretching, and pulling on their jackets. Alex sat still for a moment. How could Geri trust God to know what was best? Was Alex's dad's death the best thing that could have happened? And yet Alex felt jealous of Geri's faith and of Heidi's. They seemed so confident about what they believed—that God really was in control.

"I wish I could feel that way," Alex muttered

under his breath.

"Maybe someday soon you will," Heidi said.

Alex jumped. He didn't know anyone was close enough to hear him. Avoiding any more conversation, he hurried to help clean and put the popcorn machine away and then went out to wait for his mom.

Even though it was chilly, it was a beautiful night. The stars shone crisp and clear and the moon was full. As Alex looked up at the sky, he felt small. The universe was so much bigger. God, if he was really out there, was so much bigger, too. Alex suddenly found it funny. How could he possibly think he knew more than God? After all, he was only thirteen . . . almost . . . and God was older than everything!

Usually Alex hated to feel small. It scared him. But tonight, somehow, feeling small was comforting. Maybe he didn't have to know everything, under-stand everything, and have all the answers.

His mom drove up right at ten. He slid into the front seat and fastened his seatbelt.

"Mom," he said. "What did you mean earlier when you said we should rely on something bigger than ourselves?"

"What movie did you watch tonight?" she asked.

"*The Princess Bride*. Why?"

"I just wondered what had inspired the question," she answered. "Sounds like you've been doing some

FOURTH AND LONG

thinking like I have. This whole past year I've been trying to understand. Why did your father die? Why did you and Sara have to go through so much pain at such a young age? I'm finally beginning to realize that I'll never have the answers to those questions. And frankly, I'm tired of asking them. If I can just believe that there's someone greater than me who knows the answers, maybe that will be enough."

"Do you think God is that someone?" Alex asked.

"Yes, I do. I've started reading my Bible again. I didn't even open it for months after your father died. Now that I've started to go to church regularly, I feel more at peace and part of something greater. I need that. And somehow I feel closer to your dad."

Alex sensed that his mom didn't want to talk anymore. They were quiet the rest of the way home, both of them wrestling with their own thoughts.

CHAPTER:07

Soon Alex got into the groove of classes, football practice, games, and church. Okay, so he didn't actually attend church on Sunday mornings, but he went to almost every youth activity that Heidi or Raf invited him to. Glow Bowling, Putt-Putt, 50s Night—it seemed like every week there was something fun to do.

And he loved his work as team manager. Alex still wished he could put on a uniform and play the game. But he was surprised by how much he still felt like part of the team, even though he carried around a clipboard instead of a football.

Even with his busy schedule, Alex still found time to hang out with Jeff. Since they'd both be turning thirteen soon—Jeff's birthday was only three days before Alex's—they made a list of all the things they would never do again once they were official teenagers.

"Wear pajamas with feet," Jeff said.

"You still wear pajamas with feet?" Alex asked, cracking up.

"Only at Christmas," Jeff said.

"Where does your mom shop? A costume shop?"

"Forget it. Your turn," Jeff said.

"When I'm thirteen, I will never eat lima beans."

"Ugh! I made that decision when I was three," Jeff said. "It's about time you came to your senses."

"It's taken me a long time to kick the lima bean habit," Alex said. "Your turn."

"When I'm thirteen I will never again get on those merry-go-rounds on the playground."

"Those things always make me puke."

"Yeah, me too. That's why it's no big loss."

Alex was glad his friendship with Jeff was back to normal. Jeff knew Alex better than almost anyone. But still Alex hadn't told Jeff that he'd been going to stuff with the church youth group.

One Friday afternoon Jeff asked Alex what he was doing on Saturday. Alex just shrugged and mumbled something.

"What?" Jeff asked.

"I said I'm going to game night at Heidi's church." Alex wasn't sure what Jeff would think about him going back to church.

"With Heidi Hendricks? Really?" Jeff asked.

Alex felt defensive. Sure, Heidi seemed a little

strange at first, but she was really a lot of fun. "Yeah, with Heidi Hendricks. Is there a problem?"

"Do you *like* her or something?" Jeff asked.

"We're friends, but that's all." When Jeff raised his eyebrows, Alex said, "Really. I mean it."

"That's cool. I was just wondering."

They were quiet for a minute. Then Jeff said, "Do you think it would be okay if I went with you?"

"Fine by me," Alex said, not sure it really was. Alex had been enjoying his time with the kids at church, but he wasn't sure he was ready for his school world to collide with his church world.

Alex's mom picked Jeff up on the way. "I think I should get a commission from the offerings at that church," his mom said. "Something to help cover gas money." But she was smiling.

As usual, Heidi was waiting for Alex to arrive. She was walking toward his mom's car when Alex and Jeff got out. When she saw Jeff she stopped. She smiled and waved, but Alex thought she looked strange.

The boys walked over to her. "Hey, Heidi, what games are we playing tonight?" Alex asked.

"Huh?" she said.

"Games? G-a-m-e-s? It *is* game night, isn't it?" Alex said to the top of Heidi's head. She was staring at her shoes.

Heidi ignored his questions. "Hi, Jeff," she said, still

not looking up. "I'm . . . uh . . . surprised to see you."

Alex looked at Jeff to see if he noticed how strangely Heidi was acting. To his surprise, Jeff had also developed a sudden fascination with his footwear.

"Yeah, me too," Jeff said.

"You're surprised to see yourself?" Alex asked.

"No, I mean. Yeah. I mean. Hi, Heidi," Jeff stammered.

If Alex hadn't known better, he would have thought that Jeff and Heidi might actually *like* each other. But how could they? Jeff thought Heidi was a freak, and they hardly knew each other.

The three of them headed for the gym, where carnival music filled the air. Decorated like an old-fashioned country picnic, a white picket fence leaned against the front of the stage and some oak barrels were scattered around the floor. It really dressed up the old place.

"Ladies and Gentlemen, boys and girls," Geri announced. "Get your partners and step right up for our evening's first event—the three-legged race."

Their youth leader was dressed in an 1800s long pink dress and wearing an outrageous black wig covered by a big pink hat tied with ribbons.

"You look like you just stepped off a covered wagon," Alex teased.

"Why thank you, sir!" Geri smiled and snapped

open a folding fan before moving away.

For the first time, Alex was truly glad Jeff had come. Who else here would Alex even consider running a three-legged race with. He turned to look for Jeff, only to see him standing next to Heidi, tying their feet together with a strip of cloth.

Raf sauntered up to Alex. "Wanna race with me?"

"Sure. Where's Keisha?" Alex asked.

"At her sister's wedding," Raf said. "Come on. Let's win this thing!"

Geri stood at the starting line, holding a cap gun.

"Ready. Set. Go!" At the sound of its pop, the racers took off. Alex did his best, but because Raf was so much taller, they wobbled violently from side to side. About halfway down the course, they both fell face forward. Alex was nervous that Raf would be mad, but Raf rolled on the floor, laughing hysterically. They looked at one another, and Alex burst out laughing.

To Alex's amazement, Jeff and Heidi crossed the finish line first! In fact, they were the *only* ones to make it to the finish line without falling down.

"Congratulations," Alex said to Jeff and Heidi after he and Raf had gotten untied. "You guys make a great team."

Alex was only kidding, but Jeff and Heidi both turned red.

The rest of the night was a blast. Even though

Alex thought the country picnic theme was hokey, the games were fun and the food was great. When Heidi had her turn in the dunking booth, she shrieked loudly, as Alex and Jeff both sank her during their turns. Evidently, someone had forgotten to warm up the water.

Again, Geri ended the evening by talking about God and having a prayer time. "I hope you all really enjoyed tonight's games. I know you may have thought this was silly, but sometimes silly can be, well, delightful. Tonight I'd like to read to you from Psalm 37. In verse 4, it says, *'Take delight in the LORD, and he will give you your heart's desires.'*

"I don't know about you, but I sure know times when I've prayed to God and asked him for things that he hasn't given to me. Sometimes I get frustrated—even angry. This verse reminds me that when God doesn't seem to be listening to me, I'm probably not looking at the world through his eyes. Usually, I think only about me. But God sees the big picture. He wants us to take delight in him, not just in ourselves or the things in the world around us. When we care about what God cares about, he can give us our desires, because our desires will be the same as his."

Alex thought about his "desires." He had wanted his father to be healed, but he wasn't. He'd wanted to make the football team, but he didn't. What was wrong with wanting those things? Why couldn't God have given him his desires?

A few weeks ago Geri's words would have made him angry. Now they just made him wonder. What did God want Alex to do? And did Alex want to do it?

As Alex, Heidi, and Jeff waited for their rides, Alex's mom drove up.

"See ya, Heidi," Jeff said shyly. "I had fun!"

"Me too," she said, smiling. "See ya."

Alex climbed in the station wagon first, and then Jeff threw himself into the backseat. Alex was dying to ask Jeff what was going on with him and Heidi, but he didn't want to talk about it in front of his mom. He'd just have to wait until Monday.

Monday came and went, but Alex forgot to say anything to Jeff about Heidi. He had bigger things to worry about. This Friday was the final game of regular season. If the Fighting Ikes of Eisenhower Middle School won, they'd head into the post season. Tensions ran high, and Alex felt the pressure. So did Matt.

Matt and Alex had been working together all season. Matt was feeling more confident, and he'd gotten in some good minutes of playing time during a few games. But he'd also gotten nervous and confused and made a few mistakes.

With the big game coming up, Matt leaned on Alex

more than ever. He was even waiting at Alex's locker before school on Monday with a bunch of new questions about the latest plays. Alex answered as many as he could before he had to head off to homeroom.

"Thanks, Alex. You're awesome." Matt opened his locker and gathered up his books for class.

"No problem. You've made real progress this year. Next year you'll be a force to reckon with. You've even put on some weight."

Matt smiled, and Alex couldn't believe how good it felt to encourage someone else. Even though he was busier than ever, he realized that he didn't feel as angry anymore. Stuff didn't upset him like it had in the summer and at the beginning of school.

Practices that week were intense. Alex didn't get home until after nine every night.

"How can you be expected to get your homework done when Coach Rodriguez keeps you so late?" his mom asked on Wednesday night when she found Alex nodding off over his history book.

"It's not Coach's fault that reading history puts me to sleep," Alex said, yawning.

"Still, I'll be glad when football season is over. I don't want your grades slipping."

"They won't, Mom. I've turned in every homework assignment so far, and I'm getting good grades on my tests—better than last year even."

"I'm just concerned—"

"Mom! I'm okay . . . really."

She walked over to his desk and kissed the top of his head, before ruffling his hair.

"Don't stay up too late," she said and quietly shut his door.

Even though his mom complained about all his activities, she was great to him. She made his favorite lunches and always had a plate of food waiting for him when he came home late.

And Sara wasn't nearly as evil as usual. One morning he actually caught her making his bed for him while she thought he was in the shower. He couldn't believe it.

On Thursday night his mom came into his room again right before he went to bed. She carried a large plastic bag in one hand.

"Here," she said. "This is for you . . . for the game."

Alex opened the bag. Inside was the team jacket he'd been wanting all season. The black jacket had the school's name emblazoned in gold on the back. On the front the stitching read "Rogers, Team Manager."

"Mom!" Alex said. "This is fantastic! But you shouldn't have. These jackets cost a fortune."

"It's an early birthday present. I was afraid I

wouldn't have time to give it to you before tomorrow night, and I wanted you to be able to wear it for the game," she said.

He threw his arms around her and kissed her on the cheek. "Thanks, Mom!"

She hugged him back and then took his hand. He knew what she was thinking. The next day was not only Alex's birthday, it was also close to the first anniversary of his father's death. Alex couldn't believe it had been almost a year now since he'd seen his father.

"Your dad would have been proud of you," she said. "Now try it on!"

Alex tore open the bag and shoved his arms into the sleeves. He looked in the mirror. It was slightly too big, but he didn't look dorky. Besides, at the rate he was growing, it should fit perfect in another couple of months.

"You think I look okay?" he asked, looking at her in the mirror.

"I think you look spectacular."

Alex woke up early the next morning and lay still, trying to figure out if being thirteen felt any different from being twelve. Not really. Not yet anyway.

The halls at school were crowded with kids dressed in gold and black, excitedly talking about the game. The football guys wore their jerseys, and they almost couldn't walk down the hall without someone wishing them luck.

He couldn't help but feel a little jealous. He enjoyed his work as team manager, but he wished he were wearing a jersey, strutting through the halls, and could run out onto the field tonight. He sighed and slammed his locker door. That's what his dad would have wanted.

CHAPTER:08

That night, the football boosters fixed a spaghetti supper for the team. Alex was surprised to see his sister Sara there, helping dish out spaghetti. He wondered how she was doing. Sometimes he got so frustrated with her that he forgot she'd lost her dad too. When he got up to get a soda, she came over to him.

"Hey," she said.

"Back at ya."

"I just wanted to wish you luck tonight," she said, looking embarrassed. It wasn't often they said anything nice to each other.

"Thanks. But I'm not the one who needs luck. It's the guys out there playing."

"All the same, I wanted to give you this." She pulled something out of her pocket wrapped in blue tissue paper. "Happy Birthday." She put it in his hand and quickly walked away.

Just then Coach walked up, so Alex stuffed Sara's

present in his pocket without looking at it.

"Alex, you know how important this game is tonight. I'm going to be under a lot of pressure, so I'll be relying on you to keep an eye on the team. If you see a player falling behind, you tell me. If you see a player needing a boost, give him a pep talk."

"Absolutely. You can count on me," Alex said.

"Come on then. It's time we get going."

The atmosphere in the locker room felt electric, with everyone's nerves running high. Craig Hashimoto pulled on the same pair of dirty socks he'd worn for every game.

"Man, can't you at least wash those things?" Sam said, waving his hand in front of his nose. "They stink up the whole school."

"These are my good luck socks," Craig said.

"I don't think a little Tide will wash off the luck."

Scott Humphries looked so nervous he was ready to puke. Pretty soon, he ran to the bathroom, and they could hear him gagging.

Matt stood close to Alex, hyperventilating. "I can't breathe."

"You'll be fine, Man," Alex assured him.

"No, I mean it, I really can't breathe." Matt pulled his inhaler out of his pocket and took a puff. He didn't look very good, but Alex had seen him look worse. He figured Matt would settle down once they were on the field.

"Okay, team," Coach began. "We've played a great season. Let's enjoy this game. Play your best. We know our plays. We have the skills. Just go out there and do it."

After the speech a few of the guys gathered in a circle to pray. Coach joined them, but didn't lead it—school policy. Usually Alex avoided the group, but tonight he felt drawn to the other guys, who depended on God for help.

"Dear God," Scott prayed. "Thank you for giving us football. It's a great game. Please keep everyone on both teams safe tonight. Help us to do our best and bring honor to you and our school. And help me not to puke again. Amen."

As they headed out on the field, Alex stared up into the stands packed with screaming fans from both schools. He quickly spotted his mom and Sara and waved. Sara had brought her pom-poms and shook them enthusiastically in the air.

After the teams warmed up, the coin toss gave the Ikes possession choice. Looking to the coach for his approval, Sam Johnson, starting quarterback and team captain, chose to take the ball.

On the very first play of the game, Sam threw to Craig Hashimoto. As soon as he caught the ball, Craig was hammered by a two huge defensive backs. The impact caused him to fumble the ball, which the Blue Devils recovered and ran all the way back for a touchdown. After a successful extra point attempt, it was 7 to 0. Not a great way to start the biggest game of the year.

After the kickoff, the Ikes began their next drive attempt on their own ten-yard line. Sam looked for Craig again and threw long. He connected, and this time Craig held onto the ball and ran straight down the center of the field, escorted by two other teammates. He made it all the way to the Blue Devils' thirty-yard line before being brought down.

After a few successful running plays and another first down, Sam finally connected with Craig in the end zone for the score.

"Touchdown!" the announcer shouted. The home crowd roared.

The Ikes were in formation for Sam Johnson to kick the extra point that would tie the game. Focusing on the goalposts, Sam stepped forward into a slow run. As his foot connected with the ball, Sam twisted his left ankle and he fell hard to the ground. The ball spun wildly but somehow cleared the very bottom of the goalpost, sending the grandstand spectators into a joyous frenzy. At first, the Ikes and their fans were excited about the successful kick, but it quickly became obvious that something was wrong. Sam was hurt bad.

It took a few minutes for the game resume as Sam

was helped off the field. He had severely sprained his left ankle and would be out for the rest of the game.

On the sidelines, Coach Rodriguez motioned to Matt. "Okay, Mr. Goodman. Just stay relaxed and do your best. We're depending on you."

Alex thought Matt looked like he was ready to faint. He patted Matt on the back before the backup quarterback ran out on the field.

To everyone's surprise, Matt held his own through the remainder of the first half. At one point, when his pass to Craig resulted in a touchdown, he couldn't help but look to the bench for a show of approval by Alex and the Coach. By the halftime horn, the score was tied 14 to 14. But Matt was breathing so heavily, he could barely walk off the field.

Usually the stands were emptied out before halftime rolled around so everyone could get in line at the concession stand. Not this game. The stands were still jammed, and the crowd roared for both teams as they headed for the locker rooms.

In the locker room, Alex noticed that Matt's face was almost gray, and he was gasping for breath.

"You okay?" Alex asked.

"Fine," Matt said. Alex didn't buy it and sought out Coach Rodriguez, who was checking on the status of Sam Johnson.

"I think Matt's having an asthma attack," Alex said.

Coach rushed over to his backup quarterback and knelt in front of him. Matt was puffing on his inhaler, but it didn't seem to help.

"You okay, son?"

Coach Benson came over and looked at Matt, who was starting to calm down, but still didn't look good. "There's no way we can let him play next half," Coach Benson said.

"I know," said Coach Rodriguez.

"But he's the only quarterback we've got left!" Chuck said.

"I can go back out," insisted Sam, trying to stand on his injured ankle. Coach Benson, who was working with him, was about to disagree when Sam winced and sat back down.

"No, you can't, Sam. I won't let you risk further injury to your ankle," Coach Rodriguez said. "You're done for today."

"Then who's going to play?" protested Craig.

"Put Alex in," Jeff said. Everyone turned to him. "He's been helping Matt out all season. He knows the plays. And he's been practicing on his own. Since he's the same size as Sam, he can wear Sam's uniform."

Alex didn't know what to say. He couldn't believe this was happening.

"Do you *really* know the playbook?" Coach Rodriguez asked.

"Yeah," Alex said quietly. "I probably know it as well as Matt by now."

"Then it looks like you're our last hope. Put on a uniform, Alex. You're our new quarterback," Coach said.

Alex was going to be the quarterback in the second half of the biggest game of the season. It was like some kind of dream.

As Alex changed, Sara's present fell out of his pocket. He picked it up and unwrapped it. There was a note inside that said, "This really belongs to you. Keep it. I think Daddy would be really proud of you. Love, Sara."

It was his father's coin—the one that had been tossed during the last college game his dad had ever played. Alex couldn't believe that Sara had given it to him. He quickly stuck the coin, along with his sister's note, between the lining and the hard shell of his black and gold helmet.

The next few minutes flew by in a blur. Alex hurried to pull on Sam's uniform before halftime ended. As Alex looked at himself in the locker room mirror, and took in the magnitude of what was happening to him, he wished he could just talk to God. Instead, Matt walked over and patted Alex on the back.

"Hey, if you need any pointers out there," Matt wheezed, "I'll be sitting with the team on the bench." He gave Alex a sly grin.

"Thanks, Matt," Alex said. "You did an awesome job out there tonight."

When they went back out onto the field, he looked up to where his mom and Sara were sitting. At first they didn't recognize him. Then he took off his helmet and waved. His mom waved her arms wildly, and Sara jumped up and down.

The whistle blew indicating the start of the second half. After the Ikes kicked off, the Blue Devils began their march downfield with the ball. As Alex watched from the sidelines, the Blue Devils made first down after first down. In no time, the Devils' running back crossed the goal line with the ball raised high over his head. The extra point put the Ikes down by seven with a score of 21 to 14.

We are not losing this game, Alex thought to himself as he headed onto the field with the rest of the offense. As the center hiked the ball, Alex dropped back and looked for an open receiver. As usual, Craig Hashimoto was open and clearly the best option. Alex launched the ball towards Craig, who caught it and then miraculously broke two tackles on his way to yet another touchdown.

After Alex kicked the extra point to tie the score at 21, he heard Coach Rodriguez yelling, "Atta boy, Alex!"

It would be so awesome if Dad were here, Alex thought.

It was a real nail biter for the crowd, since the

score stayed tied through the rest of the third quarter and well into the fourth. Finally, the Blue Devils managed to kick a field goal, which broke the tie and put the Ikes down by three points with a score of 24 to 21. But Alex knew that a touchdown could now give them the lead, rather than simply tie the score up again. There was still hope.

With only a few seconds left in the fourth quarter, the Ikes faced fourth down and twenty yards to go. *It doesn't get much bigger than this*, Alex thought to himself. The team took their final timeout and the offense trotted to the sidelines for some last minute strategy.

"Guys, we only have one option, and that's to go for a touchdown and the win," said Coach Rodriquez. "We're too far away for a field goal, and we only have time for one more play. Now the Devils are going to be expecting us to take to the air in this situation, but I've got a better idea." Coach quickly diagramed a play on his clipboard and made sure everyone understood what to do. Then Alex and the rest of the offense hurried back onto the field for one last play.

As he called for the ball to be hiked, Alex acted as if he were going to run a typical pass play. But instead, he secretly handed the ball off to Craig Hashimoto as he ran right behind him. Craig then shot up the left side of the field as Alex pretended to still possess the ball and search for receivers.

Before the Blue Devils knew what was happening, they had piled on top of Alex and completely missed Craig as he ran for the touchdown!

Alex couldn't believe it. The team rushed onto the field, quickly followed by the screaming fans. Craig and Chuck dumped the water in the cooler all over Coach Rodriguez, who shook it off like a retriever running out of a pond. The noise was deafening. Horns blew and noisemakers blasted. Alex felt himself being lifted up, and his team carried him off the field on their shoulders. Alex looked up at the stars and hoped his dad was watching.

When they finally put him down, Alex's mom threw her arms around him. "Happy Birthday, Honey! I'm so proud of you!"

Then Alex saw his little sister Sara and hugged her close. "Thanks," he said into her ear. "You couldn't have given me a better present."

Coach Rodriguez came up behind him. "I told you someday you'd be glad you had a little sister."

Alex laughed. "Who would've believed it?" Sara smacked him on the arm with one of her pom-poms, but she was smiling.

People crowded around Alex to pat him on the back or shake his hand. Raf bear-hugged him, picking him up off the ground.

"Good thing I'm graduating before you make it

to high school," he said. "Otherwise I might lose my spot on the team."

Heidi was there, too, with Jeff beside her. She hugged Alex.

"You were awesome!" Heidi squealed.

"Yeah, he was okay," Jeff said with a grin. "I taught him everything he knows."

Heidi elbowed Jeff in the ribs, and Jeff blocked her with his hand. Alex noticed that their hands remained touching. They noticed him noticing, and both looked embarrassed.

"*What* is going on with you two?" Alex demanded.

"We're, uh, kind of going out now," Jeff said.

"Since when? You'd think one of you would have let me know," Alex said. But he was grinning too.

"You don't mind?" Heidi asked.

"Why should I? This just means Jeff will be getting a haircut," Alex teased.

Jeff looked panicked, but Heidi was curious, "Why a haircut?" she asked.

"When we were ten, Jeff and I promised that whoever was the first to have a girlfriend would have to shave his head," Alex said. "I'll be happy to do the job myself."

Before Jeff could answer, Alex's mom walked up again. "We need to head out if we're going to make it to the restaurant before it closes. You know how your grandparents feel about eating this late."

"Would it be okay if Heidi and Jeff came along?" Alex asked.

"It's your birthday dinner. Bring whomever you like!" his mom replied.

When Alex and the others arrived at Mack's Shack, the best burger place in town, half of the football team had already packed into the place. Everybody cheered when Alex walked in. And when the waitress brought his free dessert, everyone in the restaurant sang "Happy Birthday" to him.

"Now it's time for presents!" Sara said, handing him a gift. "I want to go first."

"You already gave me a present," he said. Alex unwrapped the package she handed him.

It was a picture frame with a drawing mounted in it. Sara was the artist in the family. She'd drawn Alex dressed in a football uniform, holding a ball as if he were about to throw it. At least, that's what Alex thought she'd drawn. He wasn't sure.

"Thanks, Sara," he said. "This is great."

Grandma Rogers was next. "I hope you like the DVD set. Your mom told us what to get. I don't even know the difference between CDs and DVDs."

Alex tore off the bow and opened the wrapping paper. "Wow! *The Lord of the Rings* trilogy! Awesome!

Thanks, Grandma!"

Alex jumped up and hugged his grandma around her plump neck. She hugged him fiercely and wouldn't let go.

"You look more and more like your dad every day," she said, kissing his cheek repeatedly. "You're still my angel boy." It was a little embarrassing. Who was he kidding? It was a *lot* embarrassing, but Alex adored his grandma.

"This is from me," Grandpa Rogers said. He handed over something soft wrapped in birthday paper.

Alex was terrified to open it in a public place. Gifts from his grandfather usually came from the underwear section of Wal-Mart. Alex barely tore open one end and peeked inside.

"Socks. White. Thanks, Grandpa. I really needed some." Alex smiled but didn't jump up to hug his grandfather. They just waved across the table.

Jeff gave him a DVD of *The Princess Bride*. "Unless I'm wrong," he said, quoting Prince Humperdink, "and I'm never wrong, you don't have that one yet."

"Nope," Alex said. "Thanks."

He opened Heidi's present last. It was a Bible, but it didn't look like most Bibles he'd seen. Instead of a fake leather cover, it was a regular softcover book. The front cover read *Teen Bible*.

"It's my favorite," she said. "It has loads of notes

and helps answer a ton of questions. I thought it was appropriate, now that you're officially a teenager."

Alex felt a little funny about getting a Bible in front of everyone. But he knew Heidi was really excited about it.

"Thanks Heidi," he said. "Thanks a lot!"

After his grandparents said an early goodnight, everyone else hung around for awhile. Lots of people who had been at the game stopped by the table to congratulate him.

"Way to go, Alex!" Raf said, stopping at the table before leaving. He was holding Keisha's hand. "I'll be watching you next year. You really came through for the team."

"Thanks, Raf!"

Keisha gave him a high-five. "Awesome! Truly awesome. See ya at church?"

"Yeah, sure," he said.

Raf and Keisha waved goodbye and moved through the crowd toward the front door.

Alex knew he should be having the time of his life. The evening had been perfect in every way, except one. His dad wasn't there. He had always thought that if he had the chance to play on a real football team, like his dad had, that he'd somehow feel super close to him—maybe even understand his father better. But he didn't. Dad just seemed far away. Alex missed him.

Besides, this was just for one game. Next week he'd go back to being team manager. Not that being team manager was a bad thing. He just wouldn't be playing on the field.

Finally they all went out to the parking lot, mainly because their waiter was making it really clear that *he* was ready to go home. Alex's mom had offered to give Heidi and Jeff both a ride, so the car was pretty crowded with them and all the presents too.

Heidi was dropped off first, and Jeff walked her to the door. Watching them, Alex felt a little bit left out. They were supposed to be *his* friends, not each other's. Maybe it was just late, but he was feeling a little down after all the celebrating. He told himself he just needed a good night's sleep.

When they stopped in front of Jeff's house, Jeff said, "So, are you really okay with me and Heidi?"

Alex paused. "Sure. I'm a little surprised. But yeah, it's cool."

"Happy Birthday, Alex," Jeff said.

"Thanks. Don't forget about your haircut," Alex reminded him.

The rest of the ride was quiet. Sara fell asleep, and Alex helped his mom carry her in to bed. Then he went to his own room. Even though he was tired, sleep wouldn't come. He heard a gentle knock on his door.

"Come in," he said.

Mom came in and sat down next to him. She handed him a present. "Happy birthday, Alex."

"Mom," he said. "You already gave me a present *and* took me out to dinner. You shouldn't do so much."

"It's not from me," she said with tears in her eyes. "It's from your father."

"What?" he asked, shocked.

"Before he died, he asked me to give this to you on your next birthday."

Alex took the gift in his hands. Sure enough, it was wrapped in birthday paper. Not very well. The paper was wrinkled and the edges stuck out. His dad had never been any good at wrapping presents. He usually gave gifts in a plastic bag from the store where he bought it. And by the end of his illness, he'd gotten pretty clumsy. So for Alex to be holding something his dad had touched, and even wrapped himself, was overwhelming. He just stared at for a minute.

Finally his mom said, "Open it, Sweetheart. He left all of us one."

With trembling fingers, Alex ripped off the paper. It was a videotape. The handwritten label said, "For Alex" in his dad's messy script.

Alex's mom wrapped her arms around him. "I love you so much, Alex. Your father loves you too. I like to think that he saw you tonight and that he's so very proud of you."

"You mean about the game?" Alex asked.

"Not just that. I think he's proud of the young man you've become and are becoming. I know I'm proud of you." She kissed him on top of his head and brushed the auburn hair out of his eyes. "Don't stay up too late, honey," she said. "Good night."

After Mom left, Alex put the cassette in his VCR and turned on the TV. The late night news was on. He pressed the "play" button, not knowing what to expect.

There was a moment of video snow, then an image of his living room couch. His father had obviously put the camera on a tripod and hit record, because after a moment, his dad appeared in front of the camera and sat down on the couch.

Alex's dad had made the video before he got really sick. Instead of the swollen arms and puffy face Alex remembered from the end of his dad's illness, the man on the couch looked healthy and muscular. It was hard to believe his dad was dead. He looked so strong.

"Hi, Alex," his father began. "It's been about two weeks since I found out that I've got cancer. I'm going to fight this disease with all I have. But if you're watching this video, it means my body lost the fight.

"I'm sorry you have to grow up without a dad around. I hate that I won't be there to teach you how to drive, or watch you go out on your first date, or help you move into a college dorm. I know your mom will do a great job. She's the most amazing woman I've ever known. But it still doesn't seem fair that you and I won't get to spend more time together."

His dad paused for a moment. Alex took a deep breath, tears trickling down his cheeks. "It's *not* fair, Dad," he said to the TV. "Not fair at all."

His dad continued. "I want you to know how proud I am to be your dad. You're so amazing. I knew that from the moment you were born. I think you'll be a great football player, but most importantly, I think you'll be a great man.

"Sometimes I think I haven't talked to you enough about important things. I've loved all our times together, throwing the football in the backyard. But football isn't the most significant thing in life. It's just the easiest one for me to talk about.

"There's something else a lot more valuable. But somehow I can never find the right words to tell you. I'm making this videotape in case I never get the chance or the courage to talk to you about this in person."

Alex swiped at his tears and sat on the edge of his bed, eager to hear more. What did his dad want to talk to him about?

"Do you want to know what the most important thing in my life is, Alex? It's not football. It's not your mom. It's not even you and Sara. It's my relationship with Jesus Christ.

"Alex, I became a Christian when I was a kid, but I never took my faith very seriously until my knee injury put me on the sidelines at the end of my college career. I always thought of God as someone to talk to when things got bad, but I didn't make my beliefs a part of my everyday life.

"Joe Rodriguez was a friend of mine in college, but I always thought he took the 'Jesus thing' as I called it, a little too seriously. After my injury I was really depressed. I skipped a lot of classes. Almost didn't graduate. Even broke up with your mom for awhile. Then Joe came to see me one day in my dorm room. He brought his Bible with him. When I saw it, I rolled my eyes. But I was ready to hear just about anything that might make me feel better.

"Joe talked to me about Jesus, and how much he loved me. That as great as football was, it was nothing compared to knowing the Lord. I didn't understand what he meant. He talked about Jesus like they were friends.

"But I started going to his Bible study group, and I learned more and more. I started reading the Bible and praying. And I began to see life after football. Your mom and I got engaged. She wasn't quite as excited about Jesus as I was, but she was willing to give it a try.

"When we first got married we went to church

a lot. But then you and Sara came along, and we stopped going quite as much. As you got older, you had games on Sunday afternoons, and it just seemed like too much of a hassle to get to church.

"Not that I really have any excuse for not talking to you about Jesus more than I did. Mostly I just didn't know what to say. I was afraid you'd ask a question I didn't know the answer to. I was stumped when you asked me when you were three if people went to the potty in heaven." His dad laughed. "I knew your questions would just get harder from there.

"What I'm trying to say is, Alex, I really want you to learn to love Jesus, too, and to be a more faithful follower of him than I ever was. Knowing Jesus has given me more satisfaction than any football victory ever could.

"You probably feel pretty mad at God that he took me away from you. I sure don't have any answers about why I have cancer. But there's a verse I learned once at church. It's Romans 8:28 and goes, *'And we know that God causes everything to work together for the good of those who love God and are called according to his purpose for them.'*

"If anything good can come out of my illness, it's that finally I have the guts to talk to you about God. Even if it's just on videotape. I hope you can really hear this and do something about it. More than anything, I want to see you in heaven someday.

"That's about all I have to say. I love you, Son. Always remember that. Take care of your mom and Sara for me. You're the man of the house now."

His dad's voice broke, and he dropped his head for a moment. When he looked up, he had tears in his eyes. "Goodbye, Son," he said, then stood up and walked to the camera. The screen went dark.

Alex didn't know what to do. He knew his dad had taken him to church some, but he had no idea how much Jesus had meant to his father.

Alex thought back on the last few months. Yes, he *had* been mad at God about his father's death and about not making the football team. But now he realized that most of the anger was gone. Now he just felt empty. Even the game tonight, which should have been the best thing that had ever happened to him, wasn't enough. And if that wasn't enough, football would never be enough.

All that he had heard about Jesus, all the lessons Geri had taught, and even all that his dad had said, came down to one thing. Jesus loved Alex and wanted Alex to love him back.

Was that the answer? And if so, what did he need to do? Alex had lots of questions, but no answers. Then he remembered the Bible Heidi had given him at dinner. She said it had answers to lots of questions. Could it answer all of his?

When Alex opened the *Teen Bible*, a card Alex hadn't seen before fell out.

"Dear Alex," the note said. "I know you've been coming to church a lot, but I don't really know what you believe. I want to tell you that having a personal relationship with Jesus is so important to me. I believe he died to pay the price for our sins, and that he is the way for us to get to heaven. Not just that, but he helps us live our lives here on earth too. If you ever have any questions, please call me. I don't care what time it is. Your friend, Heidi."

At the bottom she'd written her cell phone number. Alex looked at the clock. It was after midnight. Could he really call her so late?

What if this were real? What if Jesus really could be the answer to his emptiness? And what if he really could see his dad again someday in heaven? He wanted that more than anything.

Alex dialed the phone, and after a few rings, a groggy voice answered, "Hello?"

"Hey, Heidi," he said. "It's Alex. I hope it's not too late, but I've got some questions."

"Great," she said, sounding more awake. "Fire away."

Elijah Creek & The Armor of God

Ancient treasure lies buried in the basement of an abandoned church. And never—not in his wildest dreams—could Elijah Creek have imagined that an innocent peek into that old church would change his life forever. But it will . . .

When the treasure mysteriously disappears, the adventure to find all six pieces of the ancient armor begins for Elijah and his friends—Robbie, Reece, Mei, and Skid. Throughout their quest, friendship is tested, faith is examined, and choices determine each individual's path. Every turn in the journey highlights the inexpressible power behind the true armor of God and the commitment, knowledge, and faith needed to use the armor as a weapon in life's battles—both seen and unseen.